CAUSE TO DREAD

(AN AVERY BLACK MYSTERY—BOOK 6)

BLAKE PIERCE

BOOKS BY BLAKE PIERCE

RILEY PAIGE MYSTERY SERIES
ONCE GONE (Book #1)
ONCE TAKEN (Book #2)
ONCE CRAVED (Book #3)
ONCE LURED (Book #4)
ONCE HUNTED (Book #5)
ONCE PINED (Book #6)
ONCE FORSAKEN (Book #7)
ONCE COLD (Book #8)
ONCE STALKED (Book #9)
ONCE LOST (Book #10)
ONCE BURIED (Book #11)
ONCE BOUND (Book #12)

MACKENZIE WHITE MYSTERY SERIES
BEFORE HE KILLS (Book #1)
BEFORE HE SEES (Book #2)
BEFORE HE COVETS (Book #3)
BEFORE HE TAKES (Book #4)
BEFORE HE NEEDS (Book #5)
BEFORE HE FEELS (Book #6)
BEFORE HE SINS (Book #7)
BEFORE HE HUNTS (Book #8)

AVERY BLACK MYSTERY SERIES
CAUSE TO KILL (Book #1)
CAUSE TO RUN (Book #2)
CAUSE TO HIDE (Book #3)
CAUSE TO FEAR (Book #4)
CAUSE TO SAVE (Book #5)
CAUSE TO DREAD (Book #6)

KERI LOCKE MYSTERY SERIES
A TRACE OF DEATH (Book #1)
A TRACE OF MUDER (Book #2)
A TRACE OF VICE (Book #3)
A TRACE OF CRIME (Book #4)
A TRACE OF HOPE (Book #5)

PROLOGUE

For a man named Rosie, there was nothing delicate or pretty about him. Roosevelt "Rosie" Dobbs marched up to the front porch of Apartment 2B with his usual awkward gait—and had anyone been nearby, they might have heard him cursing under his breath, a string of obscenities that followed him like a shadow.

With a ham-sized fist, Rosie hammered on the door. With each strike, he saw the face of the man who lived in 2B. A pretentious prick named Alfred Lawnbrook—the type who always thought he was better than anyone even though he lived in a second-rate apartment in one of the worst parts of the city. He'd never paid his rent on time, always at least a week late for the two years he'd been living in the apartment. This time, three weeks had gone by. And Rosie was tired of it. If Lawnbrook didn't have his rent by the end of the day, Rosie was going to kick him out.

It was Saturday, just after nine in the morning. Lawnbrook's car was parked in its usual spot, so Rosie knew he was home. Still, despite the hammering, Al Lawnbrook did not answer the door.

Rosie gave one last violent slam against the door with his fist and then used his voice as well. "Lawnbrook, get your ass out here! And you best have your rent in your hand when you open the door."

Rosie tried to be patient. He waited a full ten seconds before he called out again. "Lawnbrook!"

When there was still no answer, Rosie unhooked the huge ring of keys he carried on a carabiner on his hip. He thumbed expertly through them to the one labeled 2B. Without another warning, Rosie drove the key into the lock, turned the knob, and entered the apartment.

"Alfred Lawnbrook! It's Rosie Dobbs, your landlord. You're three weeks late and—"

But Rosie knew right away that he was not going to get an answer. There was a stillness and quiet about the place that let him know that Lawnbrook wasn't home.

No, that's not quite it, Rosie thought. *It's something else...something feels off. Sort of stale and...well,* wrong.

Rosie took a few steps further into the apartment, stopping when he came to the center of the living room.

That's when he noticed the smell.

1

At first, it reminded him of potatoes that had gone bad. But there was something different about it, something more subtle.

"Lawnbrook?" he called out again, but this time there was a wave of fear in his voice.

Again, there was no answer...not that Rosie had been expecting one. He walked through the living room and peered into the kitchen, thinking maybe some food had been left out and started to spoil. But the kitchen was fairly clean and, because if its small size, it was evident that there was nothing amiss.

Call the cops, some wiser part of Rosie said. *You know something is wrong here so call the cops and wash your hands of it.*

But curiosity is a hell of a drug and Rosie was not able to turn away. He started down the hallway and some sick intuition cast his eyes directly toward the bedroom door. Several steps down the hallway, the smell evolved into something nastier and he knew right away what he was walking toward. But still, he could not stop now. He had to know...had to see.

Al Lawnbrook's bedroom was in a mild state of disarray. A few items had been knocked from his nightstand: wallet, book, framed picture. The plastic blinds in the window sat slightly askew, the bottom folds bent.

And here, the smell was worse. It wasn't overpowering, but it was certainly not something Rosie wanted to breathe in much longer.

The bed was empty and there was nothing to be seen in the space between the dresser and the wall. With a lump in his throat, Rosie turned to the closet. The door was closed and that was somehow worse than the smell. Still, his morbid curiosity pushed him and Rosie found himself heading to the closet. He reached out and touched the knob and for a moment he thought he could actually *feel* the terrible smell, sticky and warm.

Before he turned the knob, he saw something out of the corner of his eye. He looked down to his feet, thinking his nerves were just wrecked and playing tricks on him. But no...he *had* seen something.

Two spiders came rushing out from under the door. They were both rather large, one the size of a quarter and the other so large it barely fit through the crack. Rosie jumped back in surprise with a little scream escaping his throat. The spiders scurried under the bed and when he turned to look at them, he saw a few spiders clinging to the bed as well. Most of them were small, but there was one the size of a postage stamp scurrying along the pillow.

2

Adrenaline pushed him on. Rosie grabbed the knob, turned it, and pulled it open.

He tried to scream but his lungs seemed paralyzed. Nothing more than a dry noise came from his throat as he slowly backed away from what he saw in the closet.

Alfred Lawnbrook was splayed out in the back corner of the closet. His body was pale and motionless.

It was also almost entirely covered in spiders.

There were several thick strands of web on him. One along his right arm was so thick that Rosie could not see his skin. Most of the spiders were small and seemed almost harmless, but, like the ones he'd seen so far, there were large ones mixed in as well. As Rosie stared in horror, a spider the size of a golf ball went parading across Lawnbrook's forehead. Another smaller one scrambled up over his bottom lip.

That's what broke Rosie out of his frozen state. He nearly tripped over his own feet as he went blazing out of the room, shrieking, swatting at the back of his neck, feeling as if there were millions of spiders crawling all over him.

CHAPTER ONE

Two months earlier…

As Avery Black opened one of the many boxes still scattered around her new home, she wondered why she had waited so long to move away from the city. She did not miss it at all and was actually starting to resent the fact that she had wasted so much time there.

She peeked inside the box, hoping to find her iPod. She had not labeled anything when she had left her Boston apartment. She'd hastily thrown everything into a series of boxes and moved out in the course of a day. That was three weeks ago and she still had yet to finish unpacking. In fact, her sheets were jumbled up somewhere in these boxes but she had elected to sleep on the couch for the last three weeks.

The current box did not contain her iPod, but it did hold the few bottles of liquor she had nearly forgotten about. She pulled a tumbler out of the box, filled it with a healthy dose of bourbon, and walked out onto the front porch. She squinted at the bright morning light and took a pull from her bourbon. After enjoying the burn of it, she took another. She then checked her watch and saw that it was barely after ten in the morning.

She shrugged and plopped down in the old rocking chair that had been on the porch when she'd brought the place. She looked out at her new surroundings and was warmly reassured that she could live out the rest of her life here quite comfortably.

The house wasn't quite a cabin but had that sort of rustic feel to it. It was a simple one-story place with a modern interior. In terms of a mailing address, she was close to Walden Pond but just far enough off the beaten track to also be considered "in the middle of nowhere." Her nearest neighbor was half a mile away and all she could see beyond her front porch and the rear kitchen window were trees.

No horns blaring. No busy pedestrians in a hurry while glaring at their phones. No traffic. No constant smell of gasoline and exhaust or the droning of engines.

She downed another gulp of her morning bourbon and listened to her surroundings. Nothing. Absolutely nothing. Well, that wasn't necessarily true. She could hear two birds calling back and forth

4

and the slight creaking of the trees as a chilly late-fall breeze passed through.

She'd tried her best to get Rose to come out here with her. Her daughter had been through a lot and God only knew that staying in the city was not going to help her heal. But Rose had refused. Rose had actually *vehemently* refused. After the smoke of the last case had cleared, Rose had needed somewhere to place the blame for the death of her father. And, as usual, that blame had fallen at Avery's feet.

As much as it hurt, Avery understood it; she would have behaved the same way if the roles had been reversed. During the move out into the woods, Rose had accused her of running away from her problems. And Avery had no qualms about admitting that. She'd come here to escape the memories of the last case—of the last several months of her life, if she was being totally honest.

They had come so close to recovering the relationship they'd once had. But when Rose's father had died—as well as Ramirez, a man she had started to tolerate as her mother's love interest—that had all come to a screeching halt. Rose fully blamed Avery for her father's death, and Avery was slowly starting to blame herself, too.

Avery closed her eyes and finished off the tumbler of bourbon. She listened to the quiet sounds of the forest and let the warmth of the bourbon comfort her. She'd let similar warmth comfort her over the course of the last three weeks, getting drunk a handful of times, so much so one time that she blacked out for several hours. She'd spent that night hunched over a toilet and moaning over Ramirez and the future they had come so close to having.

Looking back on that, Avery was embarrassed. It made her want to swear off drinking for good. She'd never been a huge drinker but the last three weeks, liquor and wine had helped float her through.

Through to what, though? she wondered as she got up out of the rocking chair and headed back inside.

She eyed the bourbon, tempted to go ahead and obliterate herself by noon just to get through another day. But she knew that was cowardice. She had to get through this on her own, with a clear head. So she put the bourbon and the other liquor bottles up in a cabinet in the kitchen. She then went to the next box in her piles, still looking for the iPod.

A stack of photo albums sat at the top of the box. Because her mind had been on Rose while on the porch, Avery fished them out quickly. There were three in all, one of which was filled with

5

pictures from her college days. She ignored this one completely and flipped open the second one.

Rose stared up at her right away. She was twelve, on a sled with her hat covered in snow. Underneath this picture, Rose was still twelve. In this one, she was painting what looked like a field of sunflowers on an easel in her old bedroom. Avery flipped through them all until about halfway through the book, she came to a picture that had been taken only three Christmases ago. Rose and Jack, Rose's father, were dancing comically in front of a Christmas tree. They were both smiling to the point of giddiness. Jack's Santa hat was crooked on his head and the ornaments gleamed in the background.

It was like a knife to the heart, piercing and twisting and turning. The need to cry came on like a bomb. She'd not felt the urge a single time since moving here, as she had gotten quite good at stifling such things over the course of her career. But it hit her then, out of nowhere, and before she could fight it off, her mouth opened and an agonized moan came out. She grabbed at her heart as if that imagined knife really was there, and sank to the floor.

She tried to get up, but her body seemed to revolt. *No,* it seemed to say. *You're going to allow yourself this moment and you're going to cry. You're going to weep. You're going to grieve. And who knows? You might actually be better for it.*

She clung to the photo album, pressing it against her chest. She cried hard, letting herself be vulnerable for just a moment. She hated that it felt so good to get it out, to let herself break down. She moaned and cried, saying nothing—not calling out to anyone, not questioning God or offering prayer. She simply *grieved.*

And it felt good. It damn near felt like an exorcism of sorts.

She didn't know how long she sat there on the floor among the boxes. All she knew was that when she got to her feet, she no longer wanted to numb herself with something from a bottle. She needed to get her head clear, needed to get her thoughts in order.

She felt a familiar ache in her hands, something even stronger than the need to drink away her emotions. She clenched her fingers into loose fists and thought of paper targets and the long expanses of indoor firing ranges.

Her heart then started to lift a bit as she thought about the few items she had in the bedroom that she would eventually arrange and decorate one of these days. There wasn't much in there, but there *was* one certain thing that she had nearly forgotten about in the haze of the last few days. Slowly, trying to encourage herself as she walked through the living room full of boxes, Avery entered the bedroom.

She stood in the doorway for a moment and studied the gun that was propped up in the corner.

The rifle was a Remington 700 that she'd had ever since she'd graduated college. During her senior year, she'd had big plans of moving somewhere remote in order to hunt deer in the winters. It was something her father had always done and, while she had not been particularly good at it, she had enjoyed it. She'd often been ribbed about it by her girlfriends and she had probably scared a boyfriend or two away in high school because of her affection for the sport. When her father passed away, her mother had begged her to take the gun, thinking her father would have wanted her to have it.

It had been passed around, from move to move, usually stowed away in a closet or under a bed. Two days after moving into this house, she'd taken it to a local gun dealership and had them clean it. When she picked it up, she also purchased three boxes of cartridges for it.

Figuring she might as well strike while the mood had hit her, she stripped down to her underwear and slid into a pair of thermals. It wasn't *too* cold out this morning—a bit above freezing—but she wasn't used to being out in the woods. She owned nothing in camo, so she settled for a pair of dark green pants and a black sweater. She was well aware that it wasn't the safest get-up to go deer hunting in, but it would have to do for now.

She slid on a pair of thin gloves (having to dig through yet another box to find them), laced up her most rugged pair of shoes, and headed out. She got into her car and drove two miles away to a stretch of back road that led to an expanse of forest that was owned by the man she had purchased the house from. He had given her permission to hunt on his land, almost as some random footnote or bonus to having purchased the house for ten thousand over the asking price.

She found a spot on the side of the road where it was quite obvious that hunters had been turning around or pulling over for years. She parked her car there, the driver's side just barely off of the road. She then took up the rifle and walked off into the forest.

She actually felt silly, parading through the woods. She had not hunted for five years or so—the very weekend she had received the gun from her mother. She did not have the gear—the proper boots, the deer scent to spray on trees, the blaze orange hats or vests. But she also knew that it was a Wednesday morning and that the woods

7

would be virtually empty of other hunters. She felt a bit like the shy kid who only played basketball by herself and then skipped away when the more talented kids came into the gym.

She walked for twenty minutes and came to a rise in the land. She walked quietly, with the same practiced caution she had used as a homicide detective. The gun in her hands felt good, although a bit foreign. She was used to much smaller weapons, her Glock in particular, so the rifle felt quite powerful. As she came to the top of the slight rise in the land, she spied a fallen oak several yards away. She used it as a meager means of hiding herself, sitting on the ground and then scooting down a bit with her back against the fallen tree. In a reclining position, she rested the rifle next to her and looked up into the tree tops.

She lay there peacefully, feeling even more enclosed by the world than she had while on the porch an hour or so ago. She grinned when she imagined Rose out here with her. Rose hated just about anything to do with being outdoors and would probably flip her lid if she knew her mother was currently sitting in the forest with a rifle, looking to potentially kill a deer. Thinking of Rose, Avery was able to clear her mind a bit, to focus on everything around her. And when she was able to do that, her career instincts kicked in.

She heard the rustling of leaves on the ground as well as in the trees as the last few stubborn leaves clung on against the coming winter. She heard a skittering somewhere to her right and above her, likely a squirrel coming out to check the wind. Once she was acclimated to her surroundings, she closed her eyes and allowed herself to really let go.

She heard all of those things but she also saw her own thoughts start to slide into place. Jack and his girlfriend, both dead. Ramirez, dead and gone. She thought of Howard Randall, falling into the bay and probably also dead. And at the end of it all, she saw Rose…how she had been constantly ensnared in danger because of her mother's line of work. Rose had never deserved it, had never asked for it. She had done her best to be a supportive daughter through it all and she had finally reached her breaking point.

Honestly, Avery was impressed that she had lasted as long as she had. Especially after the last case, where her life had literally been in danger. And it hadn't been the first time.

The snap of a twig from behind her broke Avery from her thoughts. Her eyes snapped open and she was once again staring up into the mostly stripped branches overhead. She slowly reached for the Remington as yet another soft shuffling noise sounded out somewhere behind her.

She brought the rifle to her and slowly readied it. She moved with expert stealth as she raised herself to her elbows. She breathed in and out slowly, making sure not to so much as blow a nearby leaf askew. Her eyes scanned the area below the little rise she was hiding on. She spotted the deer to the west, about seventy yards away. It was a buck, an eight-pointer from what she could tell. It was nothing sizeable, but it was something, at least. She spotted another one further ahead of it but it was partially covered by two trees.

She brought herself up a bit more, steadying the rifle on the side of the fallen oak. She flexed her finger as it found the trigger and firmed up her grip on the stock. She took aim and found it a bit more difficult than she had anticipated. When she lined the crosshairs up and had a shot, she took it.

The rifle's crack as the shot was fired filled the forest. The recoil was noticeable but very slight. The moment she fired, she knew she'd be off to the right; her elbow had slipped in its positioning on the tree as she had pulled the trigger.

But she did not get to see the buck make its escape.

When the sound of the gunshot filled her ears and the woods, something in her mind seemed to tremble and then freeze. For a paralyzing moment, she could not move. And in that moment, she was not in the forest, having failed to take down a deer. Instead, she was standing in Jack's living room. There was blood everywhere. Both he and his girlfriend had been killed. She had not been able to stop it and, as such, she felt like *she* had killed them. Rose was right. It *was* her fault. She could have stopped it if she'd been faster—if she'd been better.

The blood glistened red and Jack's eyes looked at her, dead and seeming to plead. *Please,* they said. *Please, take it back. Make it right.*

Avery dropped the rifle. The clatter of it on the ground broke her out of her fugue and once again, she found herself openly weeping. The tears came, hot and flowing. They felt like little trails of fire down her otherwise chilled face.

"It's my fault," she said to the forest. "It was my fault. All of it."

Not just Jack and his girlfriend…no. Ramirez, too. And everyone else she had been unable to save. She should have been better, always better.

9

She saw the picture of Jack and Rose in front of the Christmas tree in her mind's eye. She curled up into a ball by the fallen oak and started to shake.

No, she thought. *Not now, not here. Get your shit together, Avery.*

She fought the surge of emotions off and swallowed it down. It wasn't too hard. She had, after all, gotten quite good at it over the last decade or so. She slowly got to her feet, picking the rifle up from the ground. She cast only the slightest of glances back toward where the two deer had been. There was no regret in missing the shot at all. She simply didn't care.

She turned back the way she had come, carrying the rifle over her shoulder and a decade's worth of guilt and failure in her heart.

*

On her way back to the house, Avery supposed it was a good thing she hadn't killed the deer. She had no idea how she would have gotten it out of the forest. Drag it back to her car? Bungee cord it to the top of her car and slowly drive back home? She knew enough about hunting to know that it was illegal to leave a kill just sitting to rot in the woods.

Any other time, she might have found the image of a deer affixed to the top of her car hilarious. But she currently found it nothing more than another oversight. Just something else she had not properly thought through.

Just as she was about turn onto her road, the chirping of her cell phone broke her out of her funk. She grabbed it from the console and saw a number she did not recognize, but an area code that she had seen for most of her life. The call was coming from Boston.

She answered it skeptically, her career teaching her that calls from unknown numbers could often lead to trouble. "Hello?"

"Hi, is this Ms. Black? Ms. Avery Black?" a male voice asked.

"This is she. Who is this?"

"My name is Gary King. I'm the landlord for the place your daughter is staying. She has you listed as a next of kin on her paperwork and—"

"Is Rose okay?" Avery asked.

"As far as I know, yes. But I'm calling because of a few different things. First of all, she's behind on her rent. It's two weeks late and it's the second time in three months. I try to go by there and talk to her about it but she never answers the door. And she won't return my calls."

"Certainly you don't need me to work on that," Avery said. "Rose is a grown woman and she can handle getting scolded by a landlord."

"Well, it's not just that. I've gotten calls from her neighbor complaining about the sounds of loud crying at night. This same neighbor claims to be fairly good friends with Rose. She says Rose has not seemed herself lately. Says she keeps talking about how everything sucks and how meaningless life is. She said she's worried about Rose."

"And who is this friend?" Avery asked. It was hard to fight off, but she could feel herself quickly slipping into detective mode.

"Sorry, but I can't say. Legalities and all."

Avery was pretty sure Mr. King was right, so she didn't press the matter. "I understand. Thank you for you call, Mr. King. I'll check up on her right away. And I'll see to it that you get your rent."

"That's fine and I thank you...but I'm honestly more worried about what might be going on with Rose. She's a good girl."

"Yeah, she is," Avery said and ended the call.

By that point, she was less than half a mile away from her new home. She pulled up Rose's number and placed the call as she pushed her foot down harder on the gas. She was pretty sure how the next couple of minutes would play out, but still felt a stinging hope each time the phone rang in her ear.

As she expected, it went straight to voicemail. Rose had only answered one of her calls since her father had been murdered and that had been when she had been especially drunk. Avery opted not to leave a message, knowing that Rose would not check it, much less return the call.

She parked in her driveway, leaving the engine running, and ran inside long enough to dress in something a little more presentable. She was back in the car three minutes later, pointing it back toward Boston. She was sure Rose would be pissed that her mom was coming into town to check up on her, but Avery didn't see where she had any choice, given the call from Gary King.

When the road smoothed out and became less curvy, Avery increased her speed. She wasn't sure where her future rested in terms of her old job but she did know one thing she'd miss about working in law enforcement: the ability to break the speed limit any time she damn well pleased.

Rose was in trouble.

She felt it.

11

CHAPTER TWO

It was shortly after one o'clock when Avery showed up on Rose's doorstep. She lived on a ground floor apartment in a decent part of town. She was able to afford it because of the tips she got as a bartender at an upper-class bar—a job she nailed down shortly before Avery had moved out to her cabin. Her job before that had been a little less glamorous, waitressing at a chain restaurant while doing some cheap editing work for ad firms out of her apartment on the side. Avery wished Rose would just buckle down and finish college, but she also knew that the harder she pushed, the less inclined Rose would be to choose that path.

Rose knocked on the door, knowing Rose was home because her car was parked a block down on the side of the street. Even if that clue hadn't tipped Avery off, ever since she'd moved out on her own, Rose had opted for jobs with later hours so she could sleep late and lounge around the house all day. She knocked louder when Rose didn't answer and nearly called out her name. She decided not to, figuring her voice would be even less welcome than that of the landlord she was trying to dodge.

She probably figures it's me because I tried to call beforehand, she thought.

Given that, she figured she'd go with what she did best: negotiating.

"Rose," she said, knocking again. "Open up. It's your mom. And it's cold out here."

She waited a moment and there was still no answer. Instead of knocking again, she calmly approached the door, standing as closely as she could to it. When she spoke again, she raised her voice just enough to firmly be heard inside but not nearly enough to cause a scene out on the street.

"You can keep ignoring me if you want but I'll keep calling, Rose. And if I want to get really obsessive about it, remember what I used to do for a living. If I want to know where you are at any given time, I can make it happen. Or you can make life easier for both of us and just open the damned door."

With that said, she gave another knock. This time, it was answered within a handful of seconds. Rose opened it slowly from the other side. She peered out like a woman who didn't trust the person standing on the other side of the door.

"What do you want, Mom?"

"To come in for a minute or two."

Rose considered it for a moment and then opened the door all the way. Avery did her best not to pay too much attention to the fact that Rose had lost some weight. Quite a bit, actually. She had also dyed her hair raven black and straightened it.

Avery walked inside and found the apartment meticulously cleaned. There was a ukulele on the couch, something that looked sorely out of place. Avery pointed to it and gave a questioning look.

"I wanted to learn to play something," Rose said. "Guitar is too time consuming and pianos are too expensive."

"You any good?" Avery asked.

"I can play five chords. I can almost get through one song."

Avery nodded, impressed. She almost asked to hear the song but figured that might be pushing it. She then thought about sitting down on the couch but didn't want to seem as if she were making herself welcome. She was pretty sure Rose wouldn't extend that invitation anyway.

"I'm okay, Mom," Rose said. "If that's why you're here…"

"It is," Avery said. "And I've wanted to speak with you for a while. I know you hate me and blame me for everything that happened. And that sucks, but I can deal with it. But then today I got a call from your landlord."

"Oh God," Rose said. "That greedy jerk won't leave me alone and—"

"He just wants his rent, Rose. Do you have it? Do you need some money?"

Rose scoffed at the question. "I made three hundred dollars in tips last night," she said. "And I make almost double that in tips on a Saturday night. So no…I don't need any money."

"Good. But…well, he also says that he's worried about you. That he's been hearing about some things you've said. Now don't bullshit me, Rose. How are you, really?"

"Really?" Rose asked. "How am I *really*? Well, I miss my dad. And I was nearly killed by the same asshole that killed him. And while I miss you too, I can't even think of you without remembering how he died. I know it's messed up, but every time I think of Dad and how he died, it makes me hate you. And it makes me realize that ever since you got really deep into working as a detective, my life has suffered for some reason or another."

13

It was hard for Rose to hear, but she also knew it could have been much worse. "How are you sleeping?" she asked. "And eating? Rose...how much weight have you lost?"

Rose shook her head and started walking back toward the door. "You asked how I was doing and I answered you. Am I happy? Hell no. But I'm not the type that's going to do something stupid, Mom. When this passes, I'll be fine. And it will pass. I know it will. But if it *is* going to pass, I can't have you around."

"Rose, it's—"

"No. Mom...you're toxic to me. I know you've tried very hard to make things right between us—you've tried for several years now. But it's not working and I don't think it ever will considering recent events. So...please leave. Leave and stop calling."

"But Rose, this is—"

Rose broke into tears then, opening the door and screaming. "Mom, would you please *just fucking leave?*"

Rose then looked at the floor, stifling her sobs. Avery fought back her own as she obeyed her daughter's wishes. She passed by her, painfully restraining herself from hugging her or giving some last argument. In the end, she simply walked through the door and out into the cold.

But the door slamming violently closed behind her was perhaps the coldest thing of all.

***

Avery was crying before she was able to start her car. By the time she was back on the road and headed for her new home, she was doing everything she could to hold in a series of chest-tightening sobs. As the tears ran down her face, she realized that she had cried more in the past four months or so than she had for the entire span of years beforehand. First there was Jack dying, then Ramirez. And now this.

Maybe Rose was right. Maybe she was toxic. Because when it came right down to it, the deaths of Jack and Ramirez were her fault. Her ambitious career had led the killer to those she loved the most and, as such, they had been targeted.

And that same career had pushed Rose away. Never mind the fact that the career in question was over. She'd retired soon after Ramirez's funeral and although she knew that Connelly and O'Malley were leaving a back door open for her, it was an invitation she knew she'd never accept.

14

She pulled into her driveway, parked the car, and walked inside with tears still running down her face. The sad fact was that if she abandoned her career completely, her life would be empty. Her future husband had been killed, an ex-husband she had been on good terms with was gone, and now, the only survivor from her past, her daughter, wanted nothing to do with her.

And rather than fix it, what did you do? some smaller part of her asked. It almost sounded like Ramirez's voice, pointing out how she was making matters worse. *You left the city and retreated into the woods. Rather than face the pain and a life that had been upended, you ran away and spent a few days drinking yourself into oblivion. So what will you do now? Run away again? Or should you maybe fix it?*

Back inside the cabin, though, she felt safer than she had while standing on Rose's doorstep. It seemed to lessen the sting of having her daughter slam a door on her. Yes, it made her feel like a coward but she simply didn't know how else to deal with it.

She's right, Avery thought. *I am* toxic *to her. Over the last few years, I've done nothing but make her life so much more difficult. It started when I put my career over her father and then just got worse when, no matter how hard I tried, the career won out over her, too. And here we are again, at odds even when the career is gone.*

And it's because she blames me for her father's murder.

And she's not exactly wrong about that.

She walked slowly over to the bed that she had yet to fully put together. Her personal safe was there, sitting among the headboard and the box springs. As she opened it, she thought of entering Jack's living room and finding his body. She thought of Ramirez in the hospital, already seriously injured before he had been killed.

Her hands were dirty in all of that. And she'd never be able to clean them.

She reached into the safe and pulled out her Glock. It felt familiar in her hands, like an old friend.

The tears still came as she rested her back against the headboard. She looked to the gun, studying it. It or one just like it had been on her hip or at her back for nearly two decades, closer to her than any human had ever been. So it felt all too natural when she placed it to the soft flesh beneath her chin. Its touch was cold but assertive.

She let out a sob as she positioned it back at an angle, making sure the bullet would pass through at the best angle. Her finger found the trigger and trembled against it.

15

She wondered if she'd even hear the blast before she was gone and, if she did, if it would sound as loud as Rose slamming the door behind her.

Her finger curled around the trigger and she closed her eyes.

The doorbell rang, making her jump.

Her finger loosened and her entire body went limp. The Glock clattered to the floor.

Almost, she thought as her heart slammed mounds of adrenaline into her bloodstream. *Another quarter of a second and my brains would be all over the wall.*

She looked down at the Glock and swatted it away as if it were a poisonous snake. She buried her head in her hands and wiped the tears away.

You almost killed yourself, the voice that may or may not have been Ramirez said. *Doesn't that make you feel like a coward?*

She pushed the thought away as she got to her feet and made her way to the front door. She had no idea who it could be. She dared to hope that it was Rose but she knew that would not be the case. Rose was very much like her mother in that regard—stubborn to a fault.

She opened the door and found no one. She did, however, see the rear of a UPS truck leaving her driveway. She looked down to the porch and saw a small box. She picked it up and read her own name and new address in very neat handwriting. The sender's address showed no name, just a New York address.

She took it inside and opened it slowly. There was no weight to the box and when she opened it, she found balled up newspaper. She removed it all and found just one single thing waiting for her at the bottom.

It was a single sheet of paper, folded in half. She unfolded it, and when she read the message inside, her heart stopped for a moment.

And just like that, Avery no longer felt the need to kill herself.

She read the message over and over, trying to make sense of it. Her mind worked it over, seeking an answer. And with something like this to figure out, the mere thought of dying before it was solved was out of the question.

She sat on the couch and stared at it, reading it again and again.

who are you, avery?
Yours,
Howard

CHAPTER THREE

In the coming days, Avery kept touching the area beneath her chin where she had placed the barrel of the gun. It felt irritated, like a bug bite. Whenever she lay down for sleep and her neck extended when her head hit the pillow, that area felt exposed and vulnerable.

She was going to have to face the fact that she had gone to a very dark place. Even though she had ultimately been pulled away from it, she had gone there. It would forever be a smear on her memories and it seemed that even the very nerves within her flesh wanted to make sure she did not forget it.

For the three days following her near-suicide, she was more depressed than she had ever been in her life. She spent those days curled on her couch. She tried to read but couldn't focus. She tried motivating herself to go for a run but felt too tired. She kept looking to Howard's letter, handling it so much that the paper was starting to wrinkle.

She stopped her heavy drinking after receiving the letter from Howard. Slowly, like a caterpillar, she started to break out of her cocoon of self-pity. She slowly started to exercise. She also did crossword puzzles and Sudoku just to keep her mind sharp. Without work, and knowing she had enough money to last her a year without having to worry about anything, it was very easy to fall into a mindset of laziness.

But Howard's package had erased that lethargy from her. She now had a mystery to solve which set her to a task. And when Avery Black was set to a task, there was no end until it was resolved.

Within a week after receiving the letter, her days slipped into something of a routine. It was still the routine of a hermit, but the routine of it alone made her feel normal. It made her feel like there might be something worth living for. Structure. Mental challenges. Those were the things that had always inspired her and they did that in those coming weeks.

Her mornings started at seven. She'd go out running right away, etching out a brisk two-mile run through the back roads around the cabin for that first week. She'd return home, eat breakfast, and go over old case files. She had more than one hundred in her own personal records, all of which had been solved.

But she went over them just to keep herself busy and to remind herself that among the failures that had occurred there near the end, she'd also enjoyed more than a few successes.

She'd then spend an hour unpacking and organizing. She followed this with lunch and either a crossword or a puzzle of some kind. She then did a simple exercise circuit in the bedroom—just a quick session of crunches, sit-ups, planks, and other core exercises. She would then spend a bit of time looking at the files from her last case—the case that had ended up taking the lives of Jack and Ramirez. Some days she'd look at them for ten minutes, other days she'd stare at them for two hours.

What went wrong? What had she missed earlier on? Would she have survived the case had it not been for Howard Randall's behind-the-scenes interference?

Then came dinner, a bit of reading, some more cleaning, and then bed. It was an eventless routine, but it was a routine all the same.

It took two months to get the cabin clean and in order. By that time, her two-mile run had evolved into a five-mile run. She no longer looked over the old files or the contents from the last one. Instead, she had taken to reading books she bought on Amazon featuring real-life crime dramas and nonfiction police procedurals. She'd also mixed in some books pertaining to the psychological evaluations of some of history's most noted serial killers.

She was only partly aware that this was her way of filling the void her work had once filled. As this dawned on her more and more, she couldn't help but wonder about what her future looked like.

One morning, while she made her run around Walden Pond, the cold burning her lungs in a way that was more pleasant than unbearable, this hit her a little harder than it had before. Her mind was running a loop around the questions about getting the package from Howard Randall.

First, how did he know where she was living? And how long *had* he known? She'd lived under the assumption that he'd died when he had fallen into the bay on the night that final, terrible case came to a close. While his body had never been found, it had been wildly speculated that he had indeed been shot by an officer on the scene before splashing into the water. While she ran her lap, she tried to put together a trail of next steps to figure out where he was and why he'd reached out to her with a strange message: *Who are you?*

18

The package came from New York but it's obvious he's been around Boston. How else would he know I moved? How else would he know where I live?

This, of course, brought images to her mind of Randall hiding out in those trees with eyes on her cabin.

Just my luck, she thought. *Everyone else in my life has died or shut me out. It makes sense that a convicted killer would be the only one that seemed to give a damn about me.*

She knew that the package itself would offer no answers. She already knew when it was sent and where it was sent from. It was really just Randall teasing her, letting her know that he was still alive, on the loose, and interested in her in some form or another.

The package was on her mind when she returned from her run. As she stripped off her gloves and stocking cap, her cheeks pink and blustery from the cold, she walked to where she had kept the box. She had looked it all over for clues or little hidden meanings from Randall but had found none. She'd also come up empty when she had looked over the balled up newspaper. She'd read every article on the crumpled paper and nothing had seemed worthwhile. It had just been filler. Of course, that had not stopped her from relentlessly rereading each and every word on those pages several times.

She was tapping anxiously on the box when her cell phone rang. She grabbed it from the kitchen table and stared at the number on the display for a moment. She smiled hesitantly and tried to ignore the happiness that tried to peek into her heart.

It was Connelly.

Her fingers froze for a moment because she honestly didn't know what to do. Had he called two or three weeks ago, she would have simply ignored the call. But now…well, something was different now, wasn't it? And as much as she hated to admit it, she supposed she had Howard Randall and his letter to thank for that.

At the last moment before her phone would go to voicemail, she answered the call.

"Hey, Connelly," she said.

There was a heavy pause on the other end before Connelly responded. "Hey, Black. I…well, I'll be honest. I was expecting to just have to speak to your voicemail."

"Sorry to disappoint you."

"Oh, no way. I'm glad to hear your voice. It's been too long."

"Yeah, it's starting to feel that way."

"Am I to take that to mean you're regretting your far-too-early retirement?"

19

"No, I wouldn't go that far. How are things?"

"Things are…good. I mean, there's a void in the precinct that used to be filled by you and Ramirez but we're plugging along. Finley is really stepping up his game. He's been working very closely with O'Malley. I think Finley, between me and you, he took it personally when you quit. And he decided that if someone is going to have to take your place, then dammit, it better be him."

"Good to hear. Let him know I miss him."

"Well, I was sort of hoping you'd come and tell him yourself," Connelly said.

"I don't think I'm ready to visit just yet," she said.

"Okay, so I was never good at the small talk bullshit," Connelly said. "I'll cut to the chase."

"That's when you're at your best," she said.

"Look…we've got a case—"

"Stop right there," she said. "I'm not coming back. Not now. Probably not ever, though I wouldn't rule it out completely."

"Hear me out on this one, Black," he said. "Wait until you hear the details. Actually, you've probably already heard them. This one has been all over the news."

"I don't watch the news," she said. "Hell, I only use the computer for Amazon. I can't remember the last time I read a headline."

"Well, it's strange as hell and we can't seem to get to the bottom of it. O'Malley and I had a late-night drinking session last night and decided we needed to call you. This isn't just me kissing your ass and trying to convince you…but you're the only person we came up with that could maybe crack this one. If you haven't seen the news, I can tell you it's—"

"The answer is no, Connelly," she said, interrupting. "I appreciate the thought and the gesture, but no. If I'm ever ready to discuss a return, I'll call *you*."

"A man is dead, Avery, and the killer might not be finished," he said.

For some reason, hearing him use her first name stung a bit. "I'm sorry, Connelly. Be sure to tell Finley I said hello."

And with that, she hung up. She looked at the call idly, wondering if she had just made a huge mistake. She'd be lying if she told herself the idea of returning to work hadn't elicited a bit of a thrill. Even hearing Connelly's voice had made her yearn for that part of her old life.

You can't, she told herself. *If you go back to work now, you're basically telling Rose that you don't give a damn about her. And*

20

you'd be running directly back into the arms of the creature that put you where you are right now.

She got to her feet and looked out the window. She looked out to the trees, into the thickness and shrouded daytime shadows between them, and thought about Howard Randall's letter.

About Howard Randall's question.

Who are you?

She was beginning to think she wasn't exactly sure of the answer. And maybe being without her work in her life was the reason.

***

She broke out of her routine that afternoon for the first time since establishing it. She drove out to South Boston, to St. Augustine Cemetery. It was a place she had been avoiding since the move, not just because of guilt but because it seemed that whatever cruel force manipulated fate had delivered a vicious jab to her. Both Ramirez and Jack were buried in St. Augustine Cemetery and though they were many rows apart, that did not matter to Avery. As far as she was concerned, the nexus of her failures and grief was located in that one green strip of land and she wanted nothing to do with it.

That's why this was her first visit since the funerals. She sat in the car for a moment, looking out toward Ramirez's grave. She slowly got out of the car and walked over to where the man she had been ready to marry had been laid to rest. The grave marker was modest. Someone had recently placed a bouquet of white flowers on it—probably his mother—that would wither and die in this cold within the next day or so.

She didn't know what to say and she supposed that was fine. If Ramirez was aware that she was there and if he could hear what she could say (and a large part of Avery thought that was the case), he would know that she had never been one for sentiment. He was probably shocked, even in whatever ethereal place he was occupying, that she was here at all.

She reached into her pocket and pulled out the ring that Ramirez had intended to one day place on her finger.

"I miss you," she said. "I miss you and I'm just so...so *lost.* And there's no need to lie to you...it's not just because you're gone. I don't know what to do with myself. My life is falling apart and the one thing I know will make it somewhat stable again—work—is probably the worst thing I could turn to."

21

She tried to imagine him there with her. What would he say to her if he could? She smiled when she imagined him giving her one of his sarcastic frowns. *Suck it up and do it.* That's what he'd say. *Get your ass back to work and pick up what's left of your life.*

"You're no help," she said with her own little sarcastic expression. It scared her a bit that speaking to him through his grave felt almost natural. "You'd tell me to go back to work and figure it out from there, wouldn't you?"

She stared at the gravestone, as if willing it to answer her. A single tear came out of the corner of her right eye. She wiped it away as she turned away and headed in the direction of Jack's grave. He'd been buried on the other side of the cemetery, which she could just barely see from where she stood. She walked to the little path that ran through the grounds, enjoying the silence. She paid no attention to the few others who were there to pay their respects and grieve, leaving them with their privacy.

Yet as she neared Jack's grave, she saw someone already standing by it. It was a woman, short and with her head bowed down. With another few steps, Avery saw that it was Rose. Her hands were stuffed into her pockets and she was wearing a coat with a hood, which was up and covering her head.

Avery didn't want to call out, hoping she'd manage to get close enough where they could actually have a conversation. But within several more steps, Rose apparently sensed someone approaching. She turned, saw Avery, and instantly started walking away.

"Rose, don't be like that," Avery said. "Can't we just talk for a minute?"

"No, Mom. Jesus, how can you ruin this for me, too?"

"Rose!"

But Rose had nothing more to say. She quickened her pace and Avery did everything she could not to give chase. More tears came spilling down Avery's face as she turned her attention to Jack's grave.

"Whose side did she get that streak from?" Avery asked the gravestone.

Like Ramirez, Jack's stone was of course also silent. She turned back to her right and watched as Rose grew smaller in the distance. Walking away from her until she was gone completely.

CHAPTER FOUR

When Avery walked into Dr. Higdon's office, she felt like a cliché. Dr. Higdon herself was very poised and polite. She seemed to always have her head pointed slightly upward, showing off the perfect point of her nose and the angle of her chin. She was a good-looking woman, if not a bit overdone.

Avery had fought the urge to go to a therapist but knew enough about how the traumatized mind worked to know that she needed it. And that was excruciating to admit to herself. She hated the idea of visiting a shrink and also did not want to resort to calling upon the services of the Boston PD–assigned shrink she'd seen a few times over the years following particular tough cases.

So she'd reached out to Dr. Higdon, a therapist she had heard about last year during a case involving a suspect who had used her to get over a series of irrational fears.

"I appreciate you meeting with me so quickly," Avery said. "I was honestly expecting to have to wait a few weeks."

Higdon shrugged as she sat down in her chair. When Avery took a seat on the adjacent couch, the feeling of becoming a living cliché only intensified.

"Well, I've heard of you a few times just through news stories," Higdon said. "And your name has come up when new patients have come in, people you've apparently crossed paths with in your line of work. So I had an open hour today and figured it would be nice to meet you."

Realizing that it was unprecedented to get an appointment with a respected therapist just two days after making a call, Avery knew not to take the appointment for granted. And, never having been one to beat around the bush, she had no problem getting to the point.

"I wanted to meet with a therapist because, quite honestly, my head is just a mess right now. One part is telling me that healing is going to come from time off. Another part is telling me that healing is going to come from productivity and familiarity—which leads me back to work."

"I know just the briefest of details about the healing you're looking for," Higdon said. "Could you elaborate?"

Avery spent ten minutes doing just that. She started with how the last case had unfolded and then ended in the death of her ex-

23

husband and her would-be fiancé. She breezed over the part about moving away from the city and the recent fallout with Rose, both at her apartment and their run-in at Jack's grave.

Dr. Higdon started asking questions right away, having taken down handwritten notes the entire time Avery had been talking. "The move to the cabin by Walden Pond…what made you want to do that?"

"I didn't want to be around people. It's more isolated. Very quiet."

"Do you feel that you heal better both emotionally and physically when you're on your own?" Higdon asked.

"I don't know. I just…I didn't want to be in a place where people had the ability to come by and check on me a hundred times a day."

"Have you always had problems with people concerned for your well-being?"

Avery shrugged. "Not really. It's a vulnerability thing, I suppose. In my line of work, vulnerability leads to weakness."

"I doubt that's true. In terms of perception, probably—but not in the actual state of things." She paused for a moment here and then sat forward. "I won't try to dance around topics and subtly lead you to the key points," she said. "I'm sure you'd see it for what it was. Besides, the fact that you can admit to a fear of vulnerability tells me a great deal. So I think we can get directly to the point here."

"I'd prefer it that way," Avery said.

"The time you spent alone in the cabin…do you believe it's helped or hindered your healing?"

"I think it's a stretch to say it helped, but it made it easier. I knew I wasn't going to have to deal with the onslaught of well-wishers to constantly check in on me."

"Did you try reaching out to anyone during that time?"

"Just my daughter," Avery said.

"But she rejected all of your attempts to reconnect?"

"That's right. I'm pretty sure she blames me for her father dying."

"If we're being honest, that's probably true," Higdon said. "And she'll come around to the truth on her own time. People grieve differently. Rather than escaping it all in a cabin in the woods, your daughter has chosen to assign blame to an easy source. Now let me ask you this…why did you resign from your job at all?"

"Because I felt like I'd lost everything," Avery said. She didn't even have to think about it. "I felt like I'd lost everything and failed at my job. I couldn't stay because it was a reminder of how I wasn't good enough."

"Do you still feel that you aren't good enough?"

"Well…no. At the risk of sounding conceited, I'm very good at my job."

"And you've missed it over the course of these last three months or so, right?"

"I have," Avery admitted.

"Do you feel that your desire to return there is just to fall back into what your life was once like or do you think there might be some actual progress to be found there?"

"That's just it. I don't know. But I'm getting to the point where I think I have to find out. I think I have to go back."

Dr. Higdon nodded and scribbled something down. "Do you think your daughter will react negatively if you went back?"

"Undoubtedly."

"Okay, so let's say she wasn't in the equation; let's say Rose couldn't care less if you went back or not. Would you have any hesitation?"

The realization hit her like a brick to the head. "Probably not."

"I think you have your answer right there," Higdon said. "I think at this point in the grieving process, you and your daughter can't let one another dictate the way the other grieves. Rose *needs* to blame someone right now. That's how she's dealing…and your strained relationship makes it easy. As for you…I want to say returning to work might just be the thing to help push you along."

"You *want* to?" Avery asked, confused.

"Yes, I think it makes the most sense, given your history and track record. However, during all of this time alone, isolated away from everyone, have you ever had suicidal thoughts?"

"No," Avery lied. It came easily and without much regret. "I've been low, sure. But never quite that low."

Yes, she had omitted her near-suicide. She had also not mentioned her package from Howard Randal as she had recounted the last several months. She didn't know why. For now, it simply felt too private.

"That being the case," Higdon said, "I don't see the harm in returning to work. I do think you should be partnered with someone, though. And I know that could be touchy given who your last partner was. Still…you can't be released into high-stress situations on your own so soon. I'd even recommend you do some light work first. Maybe even desk work."

"I'll just be honest…that's not going to happen."

25

Higdon smiled thinly. "So do you think that's what you'll do? Will you see if returning to work helps to get you over this self-doubt and blame?"

"Soon," Avery said, thinking of the call from Connelly two days ago. "Yeah, I think I just might."

"Well, I wish you the best of luck," Higdon said, reaching over to shake her hand. "In the meantime, feel free to call me if you need to hash anything out."

Avery shook Higdon's hand and left the office. She hated to admit it, but she felt better than she had in weeks—ever since she had finally found a routine for exercise and sharpening her mind. She thought she might be able to think a little more clearly and not because Higdon had uncovered some profound hidden truth. She had simply needed someone to point out to her that although Rose might be the only person left in her life outside of work, that did not mean that her fear of how Rose viewed her should dictate what she did with the rest of her life.

She drove toward the nearest exit to head back to the cabin. She saw the high-rise buildings of Boston off to her left. The precinct was about a twenty-minute drive away. She could head that way, pay everyone a visit, and be given a warm welcome. She could just pull the Band-Aid off and do it.

But a warm welcome was not what she deserved. In fact, she wasn't sure *what* she deserved.

And maybe that was where the last remaining bit of hesitation came from.

***

The nightmare she had that night was not a new one but it *did* present a twist.

In it, she was sitting in a visitation room in a correctional facility. It was not the one she had sometimes visited Howard Randall in, but something much larger and almost Greek-looking. Rose and Jack sat across the table, a chessboard between them. All of the pieces remained on the board, but the kings had fallen over.

"He's not here," Rose said, her voice echoing in the cavernous room. "Your little secret weapon is not here."

"Just as well," Jack said. "It's about time to learn to solve some of the bigger cases on your own."

Jack then passed a hand over his face and in the blink of an eye, he looked the way he did on the night she had discovered his body. The right side of his face was awash in blood and his face had

26

a sort of sag to it on the right side. When he opened his mouth to speak to her there was no tongue in his mouth. There was just darkness beyond the teeth, a chasm where his words came from and, she suspected, where he wished her to be.

"You couldn't save me," he said. "You couldn't save me and now I have to trust you with my daughter."

Rose stood up at that moment and started walking away from the table. Avery stood with her, certain that something very bad would happen if Rose got out of her sight. She started to follow her but could not move. She looked down and saw that both of her feet had been nailed to the floor with enormous railroad ties. Her feet were shattered, nothing but blood, bone, and chunks of flesh.

"Rose!"

But her daughter only looked back at her, smiled, and waved. And the farther away she got, the bigger the room seemed. Shadows came spilling from every direction, descending on her daughter.

"Rose!"

"It's okay," said a voice from behind her. "I'll watch over her."

She turned and saw Ramirez, holding his sidearm and looking into the shadows. And as he so gallantly chased after Rose, the shadows started coming after him.

"No! Stay!"

She pulled against the spikes in her feet but to no avail. She could only watch as the two people she had loved the most in the world were swallowed by the darkness.

And that's when the screams began, pouring out of the shadows, Rose and Ramirez filling the room with cries of agony.

Still at the table, Jack pleaded with her: "For fuck's sake, *do something!*"

And that's when Avery jolted upright in bed, a scream building in her throat. She turned her bedside lamp on with a trembling hand. For a moment, she saw that enormous room spread out ahead of her but it slowly dissipated with the light and wakefulness. She looked to the still-new cabin bedroom and, for the first time, wondered if it was ever going to feel like home.

She found herself thinking of Connelly's call. And then of Howard Randall's package.

Her old life was haunting her drams, sure, but it was also invading this new isolated life she had tried building for herself as well.

There seemed to be no escape.

So maybe—just maybe—it was time to stop trying to escape it.

CHAPTER FIVE

Once she'd stopped the heavy drinking during the more desolate stretches of the grieving process, she had slowly replaced her alcohol intake with caffeine intake. Her reading sessions would often consist of two cups of coffee with a Diet Coke in between. Because of this, she'd started to develop minor headaches after several weeks if she went without coffee for more than a day or so. It wasn't the healthiest of ways to live but certainly better than drinking herself into despair.

That's why she found herself in a coffee shop after lunch the following day. She'd gone out for groceries primarily because she'd run out of coffee at the cabin and, having only had a single cup that morning, needed a quick fix before getting back to the cabin and finishing out the day. She had a book to finish reading but also thought she might head out into the woods for another try at deer hunting.

The coffee shop was a trendy local place, with four people huddled down behind their MacBooks throughout the shop. The line at the counter was long, even for such an early afternoon hour. The place was abuzz with conversation, the whirring of machinery behind the counter, and the soft volume of the TV at the waiting end of the bar.

Avery got to the cashier, ordered her dirty chai with two espresso shots, and took up her own place at the waiting area. She passed her time by looking at the small corkboard filled with fliers for upcoming local events: concerts, plays, fundraisers…

And then she noticed the conversation beside her. She did her best not to seem obvious that she was eavesdropping, keeping her eyes turned to the events board.

There were two women behind her. One was in her mid-twenties, wearing one of those Baby Bjorn baby slings that wrapped over around her chest. Her baby napped restfully against her chest. The other woman was a bit older, drink in hand but not quite ready to leave the shop.

Their attention was turned to the TV behind the counter. Their conversation was hushed but easily overheard.

"My God…have you heard about this story?" the mother was saying.

28

"Yeah," the second woman said. "It's like people are finding new ways to hurt one another. What kind of sick mind do you have to have to even think about something like that?"

"Looks like they still haven't found the creep," the mother said.

"They probably won't," the other woman said. "If they were going to catch this guy, they would have *something* by now. Jeez…can you imagine the poor guy's family, having to see this on the news?"

Avery's attention was snapped when the barista called her name and handed her drink over the counter. Avery took it and, now facing the television, allowed herself to watch the news for the first time in almost three months.

There had been a death on the outskirts of town one week ago, in a rundown apartment complex. Not just a death, but a pretty blatant murder. The victim had been found in his closet, covered in spiders of varying varieties. Police were working on the assumption that the act had been intentional, as half of the spiders there had been kinds that were not native to the region. Despite the abundance of spiders at the scene, only two bites were found on the body and neither had been venomous. According to the news, so far, the police were working on the assumption that the man had been killed by either strangulation or heart attack.

Those are two pretty different causes of death, Avery thought to herself as she slowly started to turn away.

She couldn't help but wonder if this was the case Connelly had called her about three days ago. A case with a very unique twist and, so far, without any real answers. *Yeah…this is probably the one,* she thought.

With her drink in hand, Avery headed out the door. She had the rest of the afternoon ahead of her but she was pretty sure she knew how it would go. Whether she liked it or not, she'd probably be looking quite a bit at spiders.

***

Avery spent the rest of the afternoon getting familiar with the case. The story itself was so morbid that she didn't have a problem finding a variety of sources. When all was said and done, she found eleven different reputable sources that told the story of what had happened to a man named Alfred Lawnbrook.

Lawnbrook's landlord had entered his apartment after rent had been two weeks late for the umpteenth time and had known something was off right away, Reading it, Avery couldn't help but

29

parallel her recent experience with Rose and her landlord and, quite frankly, it creeped her right the hell out. Alfred Lawnbrook was found stuffed in his bedroom closet. He had been partially draped in at least three different spider webs, with two different bites—bites that, as the news report in the coffee shop had said, were not overly harmful.

While an actual count was not possible, an educated guess as to how many spiders had been found at the scene was somewhere between five and six hundred. A few of them were exotic and had no business being in an apartment in Boston. An arachnologist had been called in to assist and pointed out that she had seen at least three species that were not native to America, much less Massachusetts.

So there's intention, Avery thought. *And a lot of it. That much intention points to the likelihood that this guy will strike again. And if he's going to strike again in the same way, it should be possible to trace him and take him down.*

The coroner's report stated that Lawnbrook had died of a heart attack, likely from the fear of the situation. Of course, with no one having been at the scene during the murder, there were numerous other scenarios that could have played out. No one could know for sure.

It *was* an interesting case…if not a little morbid. Avery did not fear much, but large spiders was certainly on the top of her list of Things She Could Do Without. And while there had been no images of the scene revealed to the public (thank God), Avery could only imagine what it had looked like.

When she was filled in, Avery stared out of the back window for quite a while. She then went into the kitchen and moved quietly, as if she was afraid she might get caught. She pulled out the bottle of bourbon for the first time in months and poured herself a shot. She took it quickly and then grabbed her phone. She pulled up Connelly's number and pressed CALL.

He answered on the second ring—pretty quick for Connelly. Avery supposed that said a lot, all things considered.

"Black," he said. "I honestly didn't expect to hear from you."

She ignored this formality and said, "So, this case you were calling me about. Was it the one involving Alfred Lawnbrook and the spiders?"

"It is," he said. "The scene has been combed over repeatedly, the body has been scrutinized, and we just have *nothing*."

"I'll come in for it," she said. "But just this one case. And I want to be able to do it on my terms. No over the shoulder hand-holding just because I've been through a rough time. Can you see to that?"

"I can do my best."

Avery sighed, resigned to how good it felt to be needed and to know that her life would soon feel like her own again.

"Okay then," she said. "I'll see you at the A1 tomorrow morning."

CHAPTER SIX

Avery wasn't sure what she'd been expecting when she walked back into the precinct for the first time in over three months. Maybe some butterflies in her stomach or a wave of nostalgia. Maybe even a secure feeling that would make her wonder why she ever thought it had been a smart idea to quit in the first place.

What she wasn't expecting was to feel nothing. Yet, that's what she felt. When she walked back into the A1 the following morning, she felt nothing special. It felt almost like she hadn't missed a day and was just churning out another day—any other old day, just like before.

Apparently, though, she was the only one in the building who felt that way. As she made her way through the building and back toward her old office, she noticed that the busy rush of the morning seemed to quiet as she passed by. It was almost like a wave of silence followed her. The receptionists on the phone went quiet, the murmur of conversation by the coffee pots fell silent. They all looked at her as if some huge celebrity had entered the building; their eyes were wide with wonder and their faces were slack. Avery wondered for a moment if Connelly had even bothered telling anyone that she was coming back.

After weaving her way through the central part of the building and to the back where the offices and conference rooms were, it felt a little more natural. Miller, a records and research guy, gave her a little wave. Denson, an older officer who had maybe two years left before retirement, gave her a smile, a wave, and a genuine: "Nice to have you back!"

Avery returned the woman's smile, thinking: *I'm not back.*

But on the heels of that there was another thought. *Whatever. Tell yourself that lie all you want. But this feels natural to you. It feels* right.

She saw Connelly coming out of his office at the end of the hallway. The man had caused her some pain and headaches over the years but damn if she wasn't glad to see him. The grin on his face let her know the feeling was mutual. He met her in the hallway and she could tell that the A1 captain—usually a staunch hard ass—was holding himself back from giving her a hug.

"How was it coming in?" he asked.

32

"Weird," she said. "They looked at me like I was a celebrity or something. I couldn't tell if they wanted to avert their eyes or bust out into spontaneous applause."

"Truth be told, I was worried you'd get a standing ovation for coming in. You've been missed around here, Black. You...well, you and Ramirez both."

"I appreciate that, sir."

"Good. Because I'm about to show you something that might piss you off. You see...deep down, I had this hope that you'd come back some day. But we couldn't just make the entire A1 stay on pause until that day came. So you don't exactly have an office anymore."

He explained this to her as he led her down the hallway, in the direction of her old office.

"That's not a big deal at all," Avery said. "Who got that dump anyway?"

Connelly didn't answer. Instead, he took the last final steps toward her office and nodded toward it. Avery approached the door and poked her head in. Her heart warmed a bit at what she saw.

Finley was sitting at her desk, sipping from a mug of coffee and reading something on a laptop. When he saw Avery, his face went through a variety of emotions: shock, happiness, and then settling on embarrassment.

He did not show the same restraint as Connelly had. He instantly got up from the desk and met her at the door with a hug. She had underestimated how much she had missed him. While they had never truly worked together, she had enjoyed watching Finley slowly make his way up the ladder. He was funny, loyal, and genuinely kindhearted. She'd always felt as if he were a distant brother in the workplace.

"It's good to have you back," Finley said. "We've missed you around here."

"I already went through all of that with her," Connelly said. "Let's not give her a big head her first day back."

Dammit, I'm not back, she thought. But it felt even flimsier than it had five minutes ago.

"You want me to take her out to the site?" Finley asked.

"Yes, and soon. O'Malley is going to want to touch base with her later and I'd like her all nice and caught up when he lands here. Ride her out there and catch her up on everything we know. Try to get out of here in the next ten minutes or so if you can."

33

Finley nodded, visibly happy to have been given the task. As he hurried back to the computer, Connelly motioned Avery back out into the hallway. "Come with me," he said.

She followed him farther down the hall, to the big office at the end. Connelly's office hadn't changed a bit since she left. Still cluttered but in a neat sort of way. There were three coffee mugs on his desk and she guessed at least two of them were from this morning alone.

"One more thing," Connelly said, walking behind his desk. He opened his top desk drawer and pulled out two things that Avery had missed probably more than any of the people in this building.

Her gun and her badge. She smiled as she reached out to them.

"I already filed the paperwork for you," Connelly said. "They're yours. In terms of pay and the duration of your stay, I'm handling that paperwork, too."

Avery honestly didn't care about the pay or how long she was expected to stay onboard for the case. When her fingers fell on the badge and then picked up the Glock, she felt something slide into place inside her heart.

As sad as it seemed, the badge and the gun felt familiar.

They felt like home.

***

The crime scene was six days old and, therefore, was vacant when she and Finley got there. They ducked under the yellow tape and she watched as Finley unlocked Alfred Lawnbrook's apartment door with a key he took from a small envelope that he'd kept in the breast pocket of his shirt.

"You got a fear of spiders?" Finley asked as they stepped inside.

"A bit," she said. "But that goes no farther than right here, deal?"

Finley nodded with a grim smile. "I only ask because while there were arachnologists and exterminators that came in and took care of them, there were a few stragglers. Just common ones, though. Nothing fancy."

He led her through he apartment. It was very basic; the layout and appliances told her that Lawnbrook had either been a divorcé or a bachelor. "But there *were* ones that had no business here, right?" she asked.

"Absolutely," Finley said. "At least three species. One was local to India, I think. I've got the detailed notes saved on my phone

34

if you want them. The spider expert that came out and looked the place over said that there were at least two species at the crime scene when the body was found that would have had to have been ordered from a dealer. And that it would likely have been hard to get."

"Any huge ones that you know of?" Avery asked.

"I think they said the biggest one was about the size of a golf ball. And if you ask me, that's big enough."

They entered the bedroom and Avery did her best not to start scanning the walls and floor for rogue spiders. She did a quick sweep of the room and found it expertly cleaned out. The closet door was standing open, allowing Finley to reach inside and flick the light on. He did so very quickly and then stepped back just as fast.

"Lawnbrook was slumped over in the back left corner," Finley said. "We've got the pictures back at A1 and I'm sure O'Malley would love to go over them with you. That asshole is fascinated with this case."

Avery stepped into the closet doorway. Other than a few stray threads of cobweb in the corner, there was nothing to be seen.

She then left the bedroom and started looking the place over for any signs of a break-in. Finley followed behind her, keeping his distance and letting her work. She looked for anything knocked out of place, even something as small as a picture in the living room, but found nothing. She scanned the books sitting on the small bookshelf beside the entertainment center for anything linking Lawnbrook to spiders but found nothing.

"Do we have any kind of link at all between Lawnbrook and an interest in spiders?" Avery asked.

"No. Nothing."

"Has anyone spoken with the family?"

"Yes. And I think O'Malley ran backup on that. From what I understand, they painted Lawnbrook as something of a scaredy-cat. Hated roller coasters, scary movies, things like that. So the chance that he had a thing for spiders seemed to be thrown out the window."

So if the spiders weren't here because of *Lawnbrook, why were they here?* Avery wondered. *And what sort of a person would bring them here? And why?*

The days upon days of keeping her mind sharp with Sudoku and crosswords had paid off. Once the questions started rolling through her head, she couldn't get them to stop. And it felt *good.*

35

"Do you know if Lawnbrook is still with the coroner?" she asked.

"Yeah, he's still there. The spider experts have been studying him. There were eggs found in his nose and lower intestine during the autopsy."

Avery couldn't suppress the shudder she felt at this revelation. "Feel like taking a ride over there?"

"I'll take you anywhere you'd like to go, so long as it gets me away from this place. I know they're all gone, but—"

"But it feels like they're crawling on you," Avery said with a shaky grin. "I know. Let's get going."

***

Even the hectic pace of traveling from one stop to the next to find answers felt amazing to her. It wasn't just *her* moving, but her life. She could feel the sensation of things in motion, of people and places buzzing by her as Finley drove her to the coroner's office.

She had hoped there might be an arachnologist there when they arrived, but was disappointed. She *did* find that the woman who performed the autopsy was there. And that was the next best thing. After being ushered through to the back and to the examination rooms, Avery and Finley met with Cho Yin. Yin was a petite, beautiful Asian woman who seemed more than pleased to discuss the case. Like O'Malley, she also seemed to find the case morbidly fascinating.

They met in Yin's office, a very tidy room with an ancient-looking filing cabinet in the back corner. Avery introduced herself and wasted no time getting right to the point. She already felt like she was behind because of coming on so late and didn't have the convenience of niceties.

"I suppose my first question is about the bites," Avery said. "From what I understand, there were only two."

Yin shook her head and looked surprised. "That's not correct at all. Some bad reporting on the part of the media, I think. There were three bites from spiders that could have been lethal. But there were other bites as well, mostly from non-venomous spiders. There were twenty-two in all."

"Oh my god," Avery said. "And would that be enough to kill someone?"

"Yes, especially one of the bites from the venomous spiders. There were two bites from a brown recluse, as backed up by the entomologist that was on hand during the exam. The third

36

venomous bite came from a funnel web spider. And from what I understand, that's the rare one. The family from which that spider came isn't native to the States."

"Where does it come from, then?" Avery asked.

"I don't know. You'd have to speak with the arachnologist. And you know, I must say that I can't be absolutely certain the venom from the bites killed the victim. It was something that the spider expert and I disagreed on, actually."

"Why is that? What do you think killed him?"

"Well, Mr. Lawnbrook's cortisol levels were much higher than they should have been. Essentially, he was basically terrified at the moment of his death—but the levels I saw were off of the charts. The heart showed massive signs of stress and trauma. I am quite certain Mr. Lawnbrook suffered a heart attack during his time in the closet. He was *that* frightened."

"Is the body still here?" Avery asked.

"It is. I have to warn you, though…it's a pretty grisly sight."

"I'll be okay," Avery said.

She had nearly said *I'm sure I've seen worse* but then she tried to imagine what someone with twenty-two spider bites—three of which were deadly—might look like. The imagery from what Finley had told her about eggs being found in the nostrils and intestine did not sit well with her either. Still, she felt she needed to see the body for any other signs or clues.

Yin led them to the rear exam room and methodically walked over to the rows of sliding cabinets. With a hefty pull, she drew out the slab that Alfred Lawnbrook was occupying. She stepped back, allowing Avery and Finley room to step forward. Avery approached the body while Finley remained close to the door, making it clear that he had no intention of getting any closer to the body.

Even after the care and cleaning of the morgue, Lawnbrook's body looked rough. The incisions from the autopsy were almost completely overshadowed by the swelling and discoloration of the skin. Granted, it wasn't nearly as bad as what Avery had pictured in her head but it was still rather grim.

One bite on Lawnbrook's face had caused swelling along the left side, making his eye look slightly displaced. The lack of blood flow through the body made the swelling and discoloration seem almost fake, giving the entire body a waxen glow. Avery did her best to look over the body for any signs of physical abuse. And while the slight discoloration made it hard to do a thorough search, Avery was pretty sure there was nothing to be seen.

"Thank you," Avery said, stepping away from the body.

37

Cho Yin nodded and closed the drawer. "Of course, the cooling temperatures we keep here and the exam itself altered the appearance. He looked much worse when he came in. I can send you over some of those photos if you like."

"No, I don't think that will be necessary. But thank you for your time, Ms. Yin."

She and Finley walked back outside and as they made their way to the car, the questions continued coming to Avery. She sorted them out numerous ways, loving the feel of her brain naturally falling back into what it was good at.

Sure, it's natural for most people to be scared of spiders...especially that many. But would they be scared enough to cause a heart attack? And if so...well, something about attacking someone in such a way felt personal. So maybe the killer knew the victim...which opens up a whole different avenue.

That gives us two clear paths: looking for someone with an intimate knowledge of spiders, and someone who knew Lawnbrook and had some sort of grudge against him.

"Where to now?" Finley asked as he slid behind the wheel.

Avery couldn't help but feel proud of him. He was taking charge and doing so in a way that was not overpowering. He was going to be a damn fine detective sooner rather than later.

"Back to the precinct," she answered. "I'd like to sit down with O'Malley and come up with a clear plan of attack before going any farther."

Finley seemed glad to drive away from the morgue and Avery didn't blame him. Few cases had gotten under her skin and this might be the first one to feel as if it were crawling *on* her skin. But underneath even that nervous feeling was the excitement of being back on the job—of tracking down leads and, at the end, finding a killer and bringing them to justice.

CHAPTER SEVEN

He sat at his worktable and looked at all of the pictures on the wall. It was eerie to know that he was seeing a man in the images who was no longer alive. These pictures were really all that remained of him—the pictures and the miserable little imprints on the world he had left behind.

But this was a man who had lived his life in fear. And as far as he was concerned, living in fear was no way to live.

It was a lesson he'd had to learn himself, especially when acquiring all of those spiders. He'd never been afraid of them, but to see the bigger ones and how they were actual living, breathing things…they became something altogether different.

He was sitting in his basement, a small desk lamp and the glow from his laptop providing the only light in the place. He'd just finished watching the latest report about Alfred Lawnbrook. The authorities still had no idea where to look, no clues, no leads. And that's because he had let the spiders do the work for him. In the end, he had not had to place a single hand on Lawnbrook.

Behind him, something rattled. He turned and saw the old cage sitting in the floor. There were two tree limbs and an abundance of grass along the bottom of it. The squirrel was getting finicky, darting around the cage and desperately trying to find a way out.

He went to the cage, unfastened the door, and reached in. He snatched the squirrel up carefully by its neck. The little bastard had taken a nip out of his thumb the last time he'd done this so he had learned his lesson.

The squirrel went still in his hand. He could feel its little heartbeat on the underside of his hand, thrumming away like a kick drum. This was why he had the squirrel—to watch it, to observe. They were likely the most skittish animals in the world, always afraid of something. And if he was going to better understand fear, what better subject was there to observe?

He took the squirrel back to the desk. He reached under the concave area where his chair usually went and pulled out the old mop bucket. It was filled to the brim with water. Slowly, he dipped the squirrel's tail into it. The creature went spastic right away, fighting to get free.

39

He then lowered it some more, until its back legs and rear end were in the water. The squirrel's eyes went wide and it started letting out pitiful mewling sounds. It was terrified now, fighting for its life. He was so enraptured by watching it that he lost his focus for a moment. The squirrel turned a certain way that only rodents seemed capable of, and took a bite out of the back of his hand.

He screamed and dropped the squirrel into the water. It thrashed and tried to swim to the edge, but never stood a chance.

Still raging over his bitten hand, he pushed the squirrel under. He watched it the entire time, thrashing and sending bubbles up. He held it down until it stopped moving under his hand and then he held it some more.

When he was done, he slid the bucket to the wall and checked his bitten hand. The fucker had drawn blood. He might need to get a shot.

He sighed and sat back down at his desk. Ignoring the trickle of blood from his hand, he started to tear down the pictures of Alfred Lawnbrook. He crumpled them all up and tossed them into a pile next to the mop bucket. When the wall was cleared, he looked at it for a moment, smiling. He then opened up the long drawer at his worktable and took out another pile of pictures. He set them on the table, next to a roll of Scotch tape.

With his hand still dripping blood onto the table, he began to tape these new pictures up. Pictures of his next experiment—of his next victim.

CHAPTER EIGHT

As everyone filed into the conference room for the briefing, Avery realized it was the most people she had been around since Ramirez's death. Sure, there were more people than this in the grocery store when she'd had to go from time to time, but those people were dispersed throughout the store. Here, they were all packed into one room. It felt a little claustrophobic, but much like receiving her Glock and her badge earlier in the day, it felt warmly comfortable.

O'Malley had greeted her with a handshake as he took to the front of the room. Watching him prep for the briefing made her realize just how shaken up things had become within the A1 after she had left. While O'Malley had endured his share of running things in the past, he seemed more stressed now, making her think that he had a few more cases on his plate in addition to this one.

Finley sat across from her, bordered by two officers on either side of him. There were two others in the room as well, one familiar face and a brand new one. A younger officer sat at the end of the table, a woman who was surely no older than twenty-five. She saw Avery taking mental inventory of the room and gave her a stiff little nod.

"Okay, folks," O'Malley said from the front. "Let's go ahead and get this out of the way first: we are graced by Detective Avery Black once again. She's agreed to help with this case because, quite frankly, I'm starting to feel as if my hands are tied. Detective Black's track record speaks for itself and I'm sure she'll be a huge addition to the case. Black, do you have anything to add?"

She shook her head, eager to get on with it.

"We're going to start from the top today," O'Malley said. "Retracing steps, ideas, theories, everything. We all know the details, so I won't bore us all with them. But some newer tidbits that have been basically confirmed *do* warrant mentioning. First and foremost, we got results back this morning, having checked the Boston area for pet store break-ins or large purchases of spiders. We've come up with nothing. Of course, with the accessibility of the Internet, this basically means nothing, but we can at least cross it off our list.

41

"We've interviewed the family and there are no leads at all. All we know for sure is that Alfred Lawnbrook lived a very private life. His mother has indicated that he was a bit of a germophobe and scaredy cat. Hence why he had no real friends and lived alone. Now, Detective Black, you were the most recent body out at the crime scene, having visited this morning. Do you have any details to share?"

"Nothing substantial," Avery said. "I saw absolutely no sign of a break-in, which only backs up previous reports. It means that Lawnbrook willingly let the killer in. And if the killer indeed brought the spiders with them, it makes me wonder if the two are somehow connected. Maybe Lawnbrook was expecting a package. Perhaps the killer somehow knew this and used it to get in, bringing in the spiders rather than whatever package Lawnbrook might have been waiting on. Or maybe Lawnbrook knew the killer. Right now, it's all just speculation."

"And that's what we're here to put a stop to," O'Malley said. "All alibis with the landlord, family, and the one friend we spoke with checks out. There's one neighbor we need to still speak to, but they are out of the country. Which, as far as I'm concerned, is their alibi. They've been in Spain for eight days so far and are due back next week."

"Someone traveling to Spain for that long but living in those dumpy apartments?" the young woman at the back of the table asked. "That doesn't add up."

"It doesn't," O'Malley agreed. "And that's why we'll be questioning them the moment they return."

"Do we know how long Lawnbrook had been dead before he was discovered?"

"The coroner's report says as much as five days, but no longer than that for sure. Now...let's see if we can get to the bottom of this so I can stop picturing spiders *every*-fucking-where."

As O'Malley doled out assignments for the day, Avery kicked back into puzzle-solving mode. *Somehow or another,* she thought, *the killer had easy access. They had easy access* and *they weren't afraid to carry around poisonous spiders. Maybe it would be prudent to speak with an entomologist or an arachnologist at length. If I can understand the spiders that were used more clearly, maybe it will uncover something about the killer.*

On the heels of that, there was another thought. And this one seemed to have legs to it because when it struck her, it struck her hard. *Why those spiders? To have selected such specific spiders, the killer had to have known something about the victim.*

42

As the officers got up to head out with their tasks, the young woman from the back of the table approached Avery. She had very short black hair and dark eyes. Her eyes were beautiful, the most striking thing about her. Her skin looked remarkably pale in contrast to the dark hair.

The woman smiled in an almost embarrassing way and offered her hand.

"Hi," she said. "I'm Courtney Kellaway. I came on three weeks ago, a transfer from New York."

Avery shook her hand. "Nice to meet you," she said, instantly wondering if Connelly had brought her on with plans of eventually filling the hole Avery Black's absence would leave.

"In the three weeks I've been here, I've heard nothing but amazing things about you," Kellaway said. "It's nice to finally meet you."

"Likewise," Avery said, getting up from her chair. Doing her best not to seem rude, she turned away from Kellaway and headed to the front of the room where O'Malley was gathering up his files.

"I've got full freedom on this, right?" she asked him.

O'Malley winced at her choice of words and considered his answer carefully. "Mostly, yes. Why? What's up?"

"I know that you guys have already spoken to spider experts, but I'd like to follow up on that."

"Arachnology," O'Malley said with some distaste. "I didn't even know such a thing existed until this madness. And yes, by all means, have a go at it."

"I think I'll reach out to the Boston Museum of Science. They've got that butterfly garden over there so there's got to be an entomologist on staff, right?"

"I have no idea," O'Malley said. "Why don't you find out? But I'm going to ask that you do it without Finley. I need him with me for a portion of the day."

Preferring to work alone, Avery tried her best not to seem too happy about this. Instead, she instantly took out her phone as she exited the room. She pulled up the number to the Museum of Science and started down the road for her next potential lead.

43

CHAPTER NINE

It took a few phone calls and transfers between different departments, but Avery managed to set up an emergency meeting with an entomologist. She'd had her hopes on an arachnologist but the museum did not have one on staff. So Avery went with what she could get and, in the end, turned out pleased...and a little creeped out.

Donald Johansson was a sixty-year-old man with a charming smile and a thick pair of glasses perched on his nose. When Avery knocked on the door of his office, he answered with a kind yet booming voice. Avery found herself walking into an office where every square inch of the walls was covered in photographs of different insects. She saw several spiders among them.

"Detective Black?" Johansson asked.

"Yes, that's me. And thanks for meeting with me on such short notice."

"No problem. As you might imagine, a man with my field of expertise is typically not all that in demand. So it's nice to feel wanted. Now...I'm told you have something of an emergency situation. Can I assume that it's about this nasty story in the news about the man that was found dead and covered in spiders?"

"That's the one," Avery said. "Though, please forgive me. I understand that you're an entomologist, not an arachnologist. Are you still knowledgeable in the area of spiders?"

"Indeed. Spiders and all other forms of arachnids," Johansson said. "Truth be told, you're going to be hard-pressed to find an arachnologist. However, there are some circles that lump our two areas of expertise together. As an entomologist, I know about all things related to bugs. And while spiders are not *technically* insects—they are arachnids—I'm pretty well trained there as well."

"So, what can you tell me about the brown recluse and the funnel web spider? Those were the two rarest found on the scene."

"Well, the brown recluse is actually rather common. It wouldn't be hard to find one, though maybe tricky to gather it up and *collect* it unless you were trained to do so. The brown recluse is known for having a violin-shaped mark on its back. While they *do* bite and the bite can be painful, it is very rare that it causes death.

The venom can destroy blood vessels surrounding the bite area, which can cause ulcers on the skin, but that's about it.

"As for the funnel web spider, that's an interesting one. They get their name from the funnel-shaped webs they create. I believe they are mostly found in Australia and South America, though there have been reports of them living in little clusters along the western coast of the US. Their bites can be quite deadly and they are especially mean-looking buggers."

"So you're saying the funnel web bite could have killed the victim?" Avery asked.

"Oh, for sure. As for how long it would take, I'm not certain. I'd guess no more than an hour or two if the victim was not treated promptly. Now…that is interesting, for sure. But by chance do you have a complete list of the spiders found there? Maybe I could help more if I saw it."

"I have a list, though I doubt it's complete."

She pulled up the emails Finley had sent her earlier in the day and scrolled through until she got to the one about the spiders. She pulled the document up and passed her phone over to Johansson. He looked through the list, nodding here and there.

"I see a black widow listed here. They can also offer a deadly bite but most clusters of them here along the East Coast aren't nearly as deadly as they are out west or in other countries. Still, if one bit you, you'd get pretty sick. You *could* die but it would take a while, I suppose. I also see wolf spiders listed. They are known for biting, but it's not fatal. It does hurt quite badly, though. I've been bitten by one myself."

He passed back her phone and while he still had that charming demeanor, Johansson was starting to look troubled.

"You look confused," Avery said.

"No, I'm not confused, just…well, distracted, I suppose. You see…for someone in this area to get a funnel web spider, they'd have to go to great lengths to get it. And that strikes me as odd because…"

"Why?"

"Well, I'm assuming some things about the case here, but it seems strange that the killer would get this huge variety of spiders. If you're going to torment your victim with spiders, why not just use tarantulas? They are available at most pet stores and relatively easy to care for and maintain. Not all that expensive, either."

"So you're saying it would take some time and dedication to collect all these different kinds of spiders?" Avery asked.

45

"Yes. Some of them, anyway. Not to try to scare you, but at any given time, wherever you are, there's a chance there's a spider of some type within fifty feet of you. Inside, outside, wherever you are. Almost all of them are harmless. But for someone to *know* which ones to look for and then collect them in such a way…it speaks of a highly motivated person."

"Do you know how they might go about getting a funnel web spider?" Avery asked.

"My guess would be the Internet. There are all sorts of shady deals taking place online where people can buy and sell a variety of bugs. Of course it's not legal—especially not when the bugs are dangerous—but it happens every day."

Avery took note of this, once again blown away by just how many dark and seedy corners there were to the Internet. She wondered if she could get Connelly to task someone with looking into that while she carried the investigation elsewhere.

It all comes back to someone having very specific knowledge on Lawnbrook, she thought. *Someone knew he was scared of spiders—maybe even a certain kind of spider—and used that to kill him. I've got to speak to people he knew, even if it means retracing the steps of other officers and potentially pissing them off.*

Avery stood up from her chair and shook Johansson's hand over the desk. "Thank you for your time," she said. "This is been helpful and educational."

And a little creepy, she thought.

When she was out of the office, she started to wonder if she maybe had more of a phobia of spiders than she realized. Because every time she had spoken about them at length, she couldn't help but feel as if there was a family of the damned things crawling over her skin. It was a feeling she simply could not shake, even once she was back in the car and headed back to the A1.

CHAPTER TEN

When she found Connelly in his office half an hour later, he was standing by his desk while someone from Public Relations was sitting in his usual seat. He was dictating something to her and she typed it down for him. Based on what Avery heard, they were working on an update on the case to send the press.

"Sorry to bother you," Avery said, stepping into his office. "Can I borrow you for a second, sir?"

Connelly seemed irritated to have been interrupted but said nothing. Instead, he murmured "One second" to the woman at his laptop and stepped out of the office.

He and Avery stood by the wall and something about the way he intently focused on her made her realize that he was genuinely glad to have her back. She wasn't just some bonus prize who was here to help with this particular case. He valued her and now that he had gone without her for so long, perhaps he was more in tune to that fact.

"I was wondering who interviewed Lawnbrook's family," she said.

"Miles and Mackey," he said. "They did a pretty thorough job, though came back with little to work with."

"You mind if I pull the records and maybe speak to them myself?"

"I'd rather you didn't. The mother was an emotional mess from what I understand. Besides, they did a good job. If I thought the family should be questioned again, I'd have assigned it out to someone."

"What if I pose the visit as a follow-up?"

"I'd really rather you didn't do that," Connelly said. "It's borderline insulting to Miles and Mackey. Besides, I don't think—"

"If I may," a soft voice said from behind Avery. She turned and saw the young woman from the morning briefing. Kellaway, if Avery's memory served correct.

"What is it?" Connelly asked, this time doing a far worse job of masking his irritation.

"It's been five days since anyone spoke to them," Kellaway said. "After the worst of the grieving, it's been proven that family members can be more helpful. In the heat of having just lost

47

someone, they tend not to think clearly. Maybe it *would* do some good to have then interviewed again."

Connelly looked back and forth between Avery and Courtney Kellaway. He looked as if someone had just called him a nasty name and he had no idea how to respond. Avery had to bite back a smile. She wondered if someone as fresh as Kellaway had ever dared side with someone else in such a bold way.

When Connelly's eyes settled back on Avery, she let some of the smile slip out. She also gave a little shrug as if to say: *Told ya. And she has a point.*

"If you think there's anything to be found," Connelly said, looking directly at Avery now, "then yes. I'm fine with you doing whatever you want. Just don't undermine the work of the officers that went before you in the process. Be respectful of the work they've already put in."

"Of course," Avery said.

"And since the two of you seem to be of a like mind, I want Kellaway to ride along. Let her sit in on some of that grief and see if she thinks it's still such a great idea."

Avery winced internally but she could tell that this news pleased Kellaway greatly; she did a very bad job of hiding her enthusiasm.

"Sir, I don't want to seem like we're teaming up on the family members," Avery said. "I don't want to intimidate them."

This time, it was Connelly's turn to shrug. "This might be your final case with us, right? I see it as a fine opportunity to have a bright and promising up-and-comer under your wing. Show her the ropes, how you shine, and all that. Now, if you'll excuse me...."

With that, he turned back into his office. He made an almost theatrical show of closing the door behind him.

Avery turned back to Kellaway, hoping that her annoyance wasn't showing on her face. She actually respected the hell out of the woman for daring to speak so boldly to Connelly. She figured she may as well give her a chance.

"Kellaway, right?" Avery said.

"Yes."

"Can you go pull the records for Alfred Lawnbrook's next of kin? There should be some sort of report from Officer Miles or Mackey with it. Bring them to my offi—Finley's office—as soon as you can get them and we'll head out."

"Sure thing," Kellaway said. "And hey...sorry you got stuck with me. I was just trying to help."

"It's not a problem," Avery said, already heading for the office that had once belonged to her.

And just like that, she had an unofficial partner. She felt the sting of it trying to rise up, to remind her of the chemistry she and Ramirez had enjoyed. But she pushed it down as hard as she could. She was not going to let the ghosts of the past sneak up on her in the middle of this case. She could deal with them later in some other way but for now, she was busy getting her life back into some kind of familiar state.

But as she walked back into her old office and realized that she felt like a stranger inside of it, she wondered if it was going to be as easy as she had originally thought.

∗

The truth of the matter was that Avery liked Kellaway. She knew this by the time they were in the car and she was driving them to the residence of Phyllis Lawnbrook. Avery rarely felt such a certainty about someone at first, but something about Kellaway simply clicked with her. She could imagine Kellaway several years before, perhaps Rose's age. She'd probably had one of those thin nose rings. She probably had at least two tattoos hidden under her police uniform. In college, she'd probably listened to industrial music and experimented with acid.

All assumptions, of course. But there was something about Kellaway's look that brought these images to Avery's mind. And she was usually a pretty good judge of character.

"So what brings you from New York?" Avery asked.

"Family stuff," Kellaway said. "My mother got sick. She's in a long-term care facility down here now. I'm all she's got left, so I just moved."

"How long were you on the force in New York?"

"A year and a half," Kellaway said. "I know…I'm still a rookie. So please believe me when I say that I feel very privileged to be working with you."

"Thanks," Avery said.

"No, I'm serious. There were a few of your cases that I heard about even when I was in New York. And then I get down here and some of the things they say about you—it's like working with a legend, you know?"

The praise was starting to make Avery uncomfortable. She tried to remain polite and calm, though. Besides, she remembered what it was like being in her first few years, wanting to learn everything she could from those above her.

"If you don't mind me asking," Kellaway said, "what was it like to revisit Howard Randall after busting him? I know the media gave you shit sometimes about going to him for tips, but I thought it was genius."

Avery gripped the steering wheel a bit tighter and focused straight ahead. She looked down to the GPS and saw that they had another eight minutes remaining. If she let Kellaway keep going on and on, it would be a very long eight minutes.

"At the risk of seeming like a veteran bitch," Avery said, "let's not go there. I've been back for not even a single day and I'd rather not dredge up my past cases. Especially not ones concerning Howard Randall."

"Oh God, I'm sorry. I just can't even imagine what it must have been like to sit down across from him and—"

"Stop it," Avery said, her tone coming out much sharper than she had intended. There was a stinging feeling in her stomach, the familiar pangs of anger.

Kellaway snapped her mouth shut at once. She gave a sad little nod and then looked out the window. Avery regretted snapping at her at once but at the same time, felt she deserved the release. After all, she had come back to help with this case to lay the groundwork for her future—not rake up the old hurts of her past.

Maybe the past is not something you're going to be able to get away from, she thought. *Maybe it follows you until you're dead.* It was a depressing thought, but the image of Howard's letter came to mind and she thought that it just might be true.

They rode on in silence as Avery's thoughts once again crept back to Howard's package and how he had found out where she was living.

50

CHAPTER ELEVEN

When Avery knocked on the door, Phyllis Lawnbrook answered it with a plate of lasagna in her hand. It was a peculiar thing to see at first glance, but then Avery took in the rest of the situation. Phyllis was a large woman, easily a hundred pounds overweight. She looked tired but in mostly good spirits.

After a quick round of introductions, Phyllis invited them inside. As she led them into the living room, Avery picked up enough details to understand why Phyllis had come to the door with a plate of food. There were empty bags of chips scattered around the house, several dirty dishes on the kitchen sink with crumbs and scraps of food. The place also smelled like fresh brownies. Apparently, Phyllis Lawnbrook was a stress eater.

"The others that came were just police officers," Phyllis said as she sat down on a couch that was bent to catch her rotund form. "You say you're a detective. Does that mean my son's death is now a higher priority than it was five days ago?"

"No ma'am," Avery said. "It's always been a high priority. I was called in because they wanted a different approach. As of right now, we still have very few answers about who might have done this to your son. And I hope to change that."

"Well, I already told the others everything I know," Phyllis said. She forked in a mouthful of lasagna and looked at Avery and Kellaway as if she was waiting for them to start things off.

"Do you live alone, Mrs. Lawnbrook?" Avery asked.

"I do. My husband died of a heart attack four years ago. And now I've lost my only child." She frowned and then took in more lasagna. She washed it down with a glass of what looked like sweet tea that was sitting on her coffee table.

"And how often did you see Alfred?"

"At least twice a week. He'd always come over for dinner on Friday night. Then he'd come over one more evening during the week, all depending on when his work schedule would allow."

"And Alfred worked from home, correct?" Avery asked.

"He did. Something to do with designing booklets for mechanics."

"And from what I understand, he didn't really get out much. He wasn't keen to be around other people, correct?"

"That's right. He'd been like that ever since middle school when kids bullied him about his glasses and his lisp. He had friends, mind you, but not many. He was the kid that, in high school, was in the chess club and the debate team."

"Do you know if he had any friends at the time of his death?" Avery asked. She was very aware of Kellaway standing beside her, listening intently.

"No one close," Phyllis said. "The only people I ever really heard him talk at length about were some of the people he worked with. They had weekly Skype calls to go over stuff. I think the virtual workspace was good for him. He got to socialize without having to really be around people."

"And did he ever speak negatively about the people he worked with?"

"From time to time, sure. His boss was strict and sometimes overbearing with deadlines. But Alfred was never overly mean about it, you know?"

"And how about the two of you?" Avery asked. "Did the two of you have a healthy relationship?"

"I suppose," Phyllis said, setting her now-empty plate on the coffee table. "Alfred got even more closed off and private when his father passed away. So sometimes he'd come to me with issues a young man should go to his father about. It took us into some strange conversations for sure. So yes...I'd say we had a good relationship. The only arguments we ever had were when he would push me to start eating better."

"And did he broach that topic out of concern or something else?" Avery posed.

"Genuine concern," she said. "He was afraid of losing his other parent. And believe it or not, I didn't always look like this. I started binge eating when my husband died and food has always been the thing that calms me."

"Mrs. Lawnbrook, I have another question...a strange one, perhaps. I was wondering if you knew of any pets Alfred might have had in the last few years."

"No, he never had a pet. We had a cat here when he was young and it got out one day. A neighborhood dog pounced on it and pretty much devoured it right in front of Alfred. Ever since then, he's refused to have another pet."

"So then I take it he never would have had any reason to frequent any local pet stores?"

"Not that I'm aware of. Why do you ask?"

"It all goes back to the spiders…trying to make sense of why they were used by the killer. Can you think of any link at all that your son might have had to spiders or insects?"

Before Phyllis responded, a thought came to Avery, It made her feel foolish and, for the first time since calling Connelly yesterday, like she maybe wasn't ready to come back.

You were there and you missed your chance, she thought. *It was obvious, right in front of you…and you missed it.*

"I don't know if it counts or not," Phyllis said, "but he did go the museum quite a bit. The science museum. They've got that lovely butterfly garden, you know?"

"Yes, I've heard," Avery said. "I don't suppose you know of anyone that Alfred might have gotten to know well while visiting the museum, do you?"

"I'm afraid not."

"Well, thank you for your time. Please call us if you think of anything else that might help with the investigation."

When they left the house, Avery barely noticed that Kellaway was still staying quiet and reserved. She wasn't pouting, exactly; she was simply letting her know that for now, she was not going to speak unless spoken to. And for now, that was fine with Avery. She was too busy beating herself up for not exploring this avenue when she had been at the museum earlier.

It did seem strange, though. Johansson seemed to have known about the case. And being one of the museum's entomologists, he was likely a prominent figure in the butterfly garden. Wouldn't he have seen Alfred at some point if Alfred frequented the attraction?

Probably, she thought. *But he probably sees hundreds of visitors a week. And pictures of Alfred aren't very widespread in the media yet.*

Still, it was curious…and it gave her the best lead she'd had so far.

CHAPTER TWELVE

Back at the museum, Avery wasted no time in paying a second visit to Johansson's office. However, she found it empty, the pictures of all of those insects seeming to stare at her as if they were Johansson's protectors. Vacant, the room was eerie. It was all too easy to imagine that the insects all over the walls had come to life and devoured Johansson.

"You know this guy?" Kellaway said, finally breaking her silence. She made a not-so-subtle expression of disgust as she looked at all of the pictures.

"We may have spoken recently," she said.

They left Johansson's office and used a nearby museum directory to find the location of the butterfly garden. The garden was a permanent exhibit that was located on the side of the building that allowed it to overlook the Charles River. As they approached the entrance, Avery and Kellaway found that there was currently an elementary school group touring the garden. They stayed a good distance behind as they entered the garden. Avery tried to keep her eyes out for an employee to assist but was a bit distracted by the sights.

It really was a beautiful place. The greenery was well maintained and the high arched glass ceilings gave the garden a free-floating feel. As the kids several yards ahead of them chatted and giggled, a member of the grounds crew came into view—a middle-aged man, tending to the soil along a large canopy of miniature trees and flowers.

"Excuse me," Avery said, flashing her badge in a way that, even after her three-month absence, came to her in a mechanical way. "Could you perhaps tell me where Donald Johansson would be at this time? He wasn't in his office."

"I have no idea," the groundskeeper said. "He pops in here from time to time, though."

"Is there someone around that we could speak to in order to verify a frequent visitor?" Kellaway asked.

"Yeah. That would be Leslie Vickers. She's the one leading the kiddos through the garden right now. She'll pass it off to one of her assistants at the end, though. I imagine her part is close to being wrapped up if you want to follow along."

54

Avery and Kellaway gave their thanks and once again found themselves following behind the school group. Avery looked to the front of the single file line of first graders and saw a tall and poised woman of about forty. She seemed to notice the two women walking a bit behind the line of kids but did her best not to let that distract her.

Within another three minutes, the woman—apparently Leslie Vickers—came to a stop at a space that looked like a miniature courtyard. The kids took seats on a series of benches and chairs that lined the circle, looking to her as she finished her spiel about the wonders and the beauty of not only butterflies but all of nature.

When she was done, the woman smiled at the kids and walked away as a young and far-too-cheerful assistant stepped in and started talking to the kids.

Vickers approached Avery and Kellaway with a hesitant smile. "Is there something I can help you ladies with?" she asked.

"I'm Detective Avery Black," Avery said, again flashing her badge. "And this is my partner, Officer Kellaway. We were hoping you might be able to shed some light on a murder case we're working on right now. The victim apparently frequented the butterfly garden quite a bit."

Vickers's face seemed to deflate. Avery could tell that Vickers already knew where this was headed.

"Are you talking about Alfred Lawnbrook?" she asked.

"I am," Avery said. "How did you know?"

She shrugged sadly and leaned against a nearby wooden planter. Over her head three butterflies took off in a colorful blur. "Alfred came in here a lot. Some of us took the time to know him. He was shy but once he warmed up, you couldn't get him to stop talking."

"I take it you spoke with him on a few occasions?" Avery asked.

"Oh yes. At least a dozen or so, I'd say. He always looked reflective when he came in. Maybe a little sad, too."

"In talking to him, did you get an idea of why he came here so often?"

"He said he liked the idea of metamorphosis—of how butterflies are made from lowly caterpillars. He liked the idea of changing from something that is kind of ugly and always on the ground into this beautiful creature. I never asked him directly, but I assume he had some sort of messed up childhood or something."

"Did he ever mention spiders to you in your talks?" Avery asked.

"I keep wondering that myself," Vickers said. "Ever since I saw that awful news report, I kept wondering if there were clues or some sort of foreshadowing as to how it could have happened. But I honestly don't remember him ever mentioning spiders. If he did, it certainly wasn't at length."

"What about other insects?" Kellaway asked.

"No. I will say, though, that there was one day where I offhandedly mentioned beetles for some reason. He seemed to get very uncomfortable; he got up from his seat and started sort of pacing."

"Was there ever any indication that he had enemies?" Avery asked. "Or even people he was uneasy about?"

"No," Vickers answered. "He never mentioned a girlfriend or even friends. He sometimes talked about his work and his mom. I also know his father died a while back. But he never spoke ill of anyone or like he was afraid of someone in particular."

"Do you know if there was anyone else he spoke to frequently?"

"Yes. He and Donald Johansson had quite a few conversations."

"Really?" Avery asked.

"Yes. I wouldn't say they were friends or anything like that, but I know for a fact they spoke a few times. Saw it with my own eyes."

Why would Johansson lie about that? she wondered.

"And do you know where I might find him?" she asked.

Vickers smiled and nodded behind them. "Yes, as a matter of fact. Here he comes now."

Avery and Kellaway turned to look behind them. Johansson had only just seen them and was frozen in place between two bends in the walkway along the garden. The expression on his face at seeing Avery told her everything she needed to know: he was hiding something.

Like a shark smelling blood in the water, Avery wasted no time. She headed in his direction right away with purpose in her step. "Mr. Johansson, it's nice to see you again," she said.

"Oh, yes, you as well," he said. But his tone indicated that was not the case at all.

"With all due respect," Avery said, "I can't help but feel that you were lying to me when we spoke earlier. Or, if not lying, certainly omitting quite a few things."

Johansson looked to the walkway and nodded. "Yes, I suppose I was."

56

"I hope you have a very good reason," she said. "Otherwise, I'd have to go through the trouble of arresting you in front of your coworkers."

Johansson let out a shaky sigh and nodded. "You mind coming back to my office again?" he asked.

Honestly, Avery would rather stay in the butterfly garden rather than his dimly lit office with all those pictures of insects on the walls. Still, she nodded and said, "That's fine."

He led them out of the butterfly garden and back out into Level 2 of the museum. Avery took one last look back into the garden, and then to Kellaway, who had a confused look on her face that she didn't even try to hide. Avery didn't let it bother her too much. She had a feeling that Kellaway would be more than caught up within a few minutes.

***

"Yes, I got to know Alfred Lawnbrook during his frequent visits to the butterfly garden," Johansson said as he sat behind his desk. "He was an isolated young man who clearly had many social anxieties, which is why myself and a few other employees tried to take the time to speak with him."

"And why did you not see fit to tell me you knew him when I was here a little over two hours ago?" Avery said. "It would have saved me a hell of a lot of time and trouble."

"Because I was trying to protect someone I care a great deal about."

"You mean to tell me you knew Lawnbrook outside of the museum?"

"No," Johansson said. Avery could see that there were tears welling up in his eyes, a clear indication that some kind of revelation was on the way. "But I did know someone that got to know him well. A former museum employee by the same of Stefon Scott. He was released last month. I knew Stefon well because I mentored him as he was coming up in the museum."

"And what was his affiliation with Alfred Lawnbrook?" Avery asked.

"It depends on who you ask," Johansson said. "Some would say they had something of a blossoming friendship. But I knew the truth...and I learned it by accident. The truth of the matter was that Alfred and Stefon met in the butterfly garden about a year ago and really hit it off. It developed into a romantic relationship that they tried to hide. They did a good job, except I walked in on Stefon

57

speaking on the phone to Alfred one day. I heard enough to know what was going on so Stefon confided in me. Told me how happy he was but how weird it was, too. He had no idea he was gay until Alfred showed up in his life, apparently. But he also asked me to keep it a secret. And because he had come to be like a secondary son to me here at the museum, I decided to keep that promise when you were here earlier. I do apologize for any inconvenience."

Putting aside her irritation of having been lied to, Avery continued forward. "You said Mr. Scott was released from the hospital last month. Why was he fired?"

At this point, Johansson was finding it hard to look at her. She could see the mess of conflict on his face—the battle between knowing he needed to tell what he knew battling with a promise made to a friend. Finally, still not looking at Avery or Kellaway, he answered. His voice was thick as he tried to hold back a bout of weeping.

"I knew Stefon very well," he said. "I can tell you on my heart, on my *life*, that he did not have it in him to do the sort of things that were done to Alfred Lawnbrook."

"What did he do?" Kellaway asked. "Why was he let go?"

"He was obsessed with spiders...so much so that he started taking some home with him. When the museum found out, they fined and fired him. We still don't think he returned all of them."

Avery got to her feet and slammed her hand down on the desk. "You knew someone obsessed with spiders was involved with Alfred Lawnbrook...and you thought that information did not need to be shared when I was here two hours ago?"

"I'm sorry, I—"

"Officer Kellaway, please cuff this bastard and read him his rights."

"But I—" Johansson started.

"Very talkative now, I see," Avery said, turning away from him while Kellaway dutifully did as she was asked.

Avery pulled out her phone and called up Connelly. She figured if she could get an address for Stefon Scott, this entire case could potentially be wrapped up within the hour. The pleading cries of Johansson from behind her as Kellaway applied the handcuffs seemed to only cement this notion.

58

CHAPTER THIRTEEN

Avery parked in front of Stefon Scott's one-story house forty minutes later. He lived in one of the many small brick row houses in the Bay Village area. When she had called the A1 to get an address and any information on him, she also learned that he was currently unemployed, still not having found another job in the month he'd been gone from the museum.

The timing is almost too perfect, she thought as she and Kellaway climbed the slight staircase to his front door. *He was released a month ago for stealing spiders...and Lawnbrook is killed via spiders a little more than a week ago. It's a cookie cutter timeline that seems almost too perfect.*

The door was answered not by Stefon Scott, but by a woman dressed in a black band T-shirt and a pair of sweatpants. Her hair was dyed a nearly neon red color and she wore a bull ring in her nose and a lip ring in her bottom lip. A tattoo of a large spider adorned her right forearm.

"We're looking for Stefon Scott," Avery said.

The woman—barely a woman at all from the looks of it, maybe twenty-one at most—rolled her eyes. "Who's asking?"

"Detective Avery Black and Officer Courtney Kellaway. Is he home?"

The girl nodded and took a slow step back. "What's this about?" she asked.

"For your sake," Avery said, "I hope it's none of your business. Now, where is he?"

"Still asleep," the girl said.

"It's three in the afternoon," Kellaway pointed out.

"We were out really late," the girl said. "And Stefon has been depressed as hell ever since he lost his job. He sleeps a lot."

"I need you to wake him up," Avery said sternly.

"Yeah, okay. Go on and have a seat in the living room," the girl said as she closed the door behind them.

As the girl walked down the small hallway to a bedroom in the back of the house, Avery and Kellaway moved to the living room. It sat right off of the tiny foyer, not quite in a shambles but in need of straightening up. There were books scattered everywhere, as well as printed sheets of paper all over the small coffee table. Avery checked a few of the sheets. Some were for guitar tablature; a few looked to be the beginnings of articles about spiders that Stefon had been trying to write.

"Detective Black," Kellaway said.

Avery looked to the other side of the room where Kellaway was observing something sitting by the side of the couch. As she joined Kellaway, she saw that it was a large glass case, most of which was covered by a black sheet. Kellaway slowly lifted the portion of the sheet that was covering the side facing them.

Three spiders sat inside the case. Avery was by no means a spider expert but she thought they were tarantulas—and if not tarantulas, then some variety that very closely resembled them. Two of the spiders were motionless while the third was scurrying away from the sudden movement of the sheet.

Behind them, Stefon Scott slowly walked into the room, clearly still half-asleep. "Those are tarantula wolf spiders," he said. "Also known as the lycosa tarantula."

"And why do you have them?" Avery asked.

He gave a shrug that, for reasons Avery couldn't quite figure out, pissed her off. "I've just always liked spiders. I have a few more in my bedroom. I've had at least two as pets since I was twelve years old."

He sat down on the couch and looked up at both of them. Avery could tell he was aware that things were probably going to get tense. He was trying his best to convince them that he wasn't bothered by their visit.

"We heard all about your interest in spiders from Donald Johansson," Avery said.

Stefon nodded slowly, looking to the glass case. "If you're here with me right now," he said, "I suppose that's not all you heard about me."

"That's right," Avery said. "He told us about your relationship with Alfred Lawnbrook. Can I assume you've heard what happened to him?"

"Yes," he said, nearly spitting the word out. "So I guess you're here to find out why he and I were together, right? I wasn't...I'm not...shit. I don't even know. I mean, we weren't ever really seeing one another, you know. It was just...physical."

"So then who was the girl that answered the door?" Kellaway asked.

"Just some girl I've been seeing the last few weeks. Met her online...a forum for arachnid lovers."

60

"Is that how you met Alfred?" Avery asked. She knew this was not how they met based on what Johansson had revealed but she wanted to see how Stefon would respond.

"No. I met him at the butterfly garden at the museum when I was still working there. We hung out once and I found out then and there that he was terrified of spiders. Like *terrified.* I found that interesting. So we chatted and one thing led to another and within a week or so, he was coming over and spending the night."

"You said you weren't seeing one another when he died," Avery said. "What happened between you?"

"It was a love-hate thing. He hated my spiders, thought I was weird. It freaked him out but I think something about his fear sort of attracted him to me. I think maybe he wanted to get over it or explore it. Or...and not to speak ill of the dead, but I was starting to wonder if his fear of spiders helped things along with he and I. I think knowing there were spiders on my bureau when we were in bed together turned him on. I don't know."

"And you were fired from the museum for stealing spiders, correct?"

"Yeah. Not my finest moment."

Avery was done beating around the bush. She'd already been jerked around by Johansson and she did not intend to let Stefon Scott do the same thing.

"You seem very relaxed and calm," Avery said. "Do you honestly not understand why we are here?"

"To get information about what happened to Alfred, I guess. But like I said...I hadn't seen him for a while before he died."

"You can't be this naïve," Avery said. "You have a fascination with spiders. You even stole them from the museum. You also had a sexual relationship with a recently deceased man who was tortured and killed *with* spiders..."

"Hold on," Stefon said. "Wait. You think *I* killed him?"

"It's where all the signs are pointing right now," Avery said. "Look at the situation from where we're standing. It's almost paint-by-numbers simple. So I'm going to ask you to come to the precinct with us for some questioning."

"So because I *stole* something from work, you think that also puts me in cold-blooded murderer territory?"

"I'm making no such claims at the moment. I just need you to come with us. You can come willingly or we can make it harder than it has to be."

"First of all," Stefon said, getting to his feet, "I would have never purposefully hurt Alfred. He had some emotional problems, which I suppose is why he engaged in a gay relationship when he had never even really been in a straight one—even though he swears he's straight. He just wanted companionship. He was a good guy. I would never have hurt him. Secondly…there's no way you have any proof that I did it. And without hard proof…really, what can you do?"

"Quite a bit actually," Avery said.

On cue, Kellaway stepped forward. "Hands behind your back," she said.

"Fuck you."

"That was the worst response you could have given," Avery said. She joined Kellaway and together, they wrestled Stefon to the floor. He fought against them for a few seconds before giving in completely. By the time the cuffs were on him and they had him back to his feet, he was openly crying.

"Clarissa!" Stefon screamed. "Clarissa…they're taking me! Call someone to help! And feed the spiders!"

Something about the last comment seemed hilarious to Avery but she kept her composure. She and Kellaway hauled Stefon out of the front door and down to the car. As Avery reached back to close the door, she saw the woman who had answered the door—Clarissa, presumably—hurrying toward the commotion. Something about closing the door on her, leaving her there with Stefon's pet spiders, seemed wrong. It felt like shutting her in her own tomb and Avery could not get the images of Alfred Lawnbrook's body out of her mind.

The image was still there as they drove toward the precinct with Stefon Scott screaming and crying in the back seat.

CHAPTER FOURTEEN

As they came upon the precinct, Avery saw the flurry of activity in the parking lot and around the front of the building. New anger rose up in her stomach and she let out a curse under her breath.

"What?" Kellaway asked. "What's going on?"

"The media," Avery said. "They're onto the case. And that's just going to make it harder from here on out."

"Oh," Kellaway said, staring closer at the craziness as Avery pulled the car closer.

There were three news vans parked bumper to bumper in front of the building. Several people were standing along the sidewalk that led to the front doors, reporters and cameramen just waiting for their chance to score something big for the six o'clock news. Another news van came screeching into the parking lot from the opposite direction, pulling in alongside the others.

Somehow, the media knows I'm on this case, Avery thought to herself. Not that she thought she was worthy of the attention. But she knew how the media worked. *Victimized Detective Returns to Work on Creepy Spider Case.* That or *Howard Randall-obsessed Detective Back in Action on Creepy Case.*

Something like that. Hell, she didn't even blame them. If they could spin it a certain way, it was front page news for sure.

Avery sped around to the back of the building but it did no good. There was a news crew there, too. And by the time she had parked and started to get out of the car with Stefon Scott, several of the people who had been angling for position out front had managed to race around the building. As she walked quickly to the building with Kellaway racing to keep up and pushing Stefon along, cameras started flashing and about eight people started talking at once. Avery put her head down and carried on, refusing to give in to the pandemonium.

"Detective Black, why have you come back for this case?"

"Have you come back to respect the memory of Detective Ramirez?"

"Why is this man in custody, Detective? Is he a suspect in this case?"

63

"Do you feel that Howard Randall is dead even though his body was not discovered?"

"Are there any leads on the spider case?"

Mercifully, she reached the doors. She hauled Stefon Scott through them but Kellaway was nowhere to be seen. She looked over the shoulders of the assembled crowd and saw her wrapped up in their midst. She looked scared and out of her element. It did not piss Avery off, though; rather, she felt for Kellaway. The media could be vultures and they could smell fresh blood when it was around.

She pushed Stefon toward the first officer she saw in the hallway and then stormed back through the doors, back outside. She had to shoulder her way past a cameraman and nearly knock down a svelte reporter before she reached Kellaway. Thankfully, she was not offering up any information but all the same, the reporters had managed to snare her with confusion.

"How did you manage to partner with Detective Black?"

"How long have you been on the force?"

"Is the man in handcuffs the killer?"

"Can I get your name, please?"

Avery grabbed Kellaway's arm and hauled her through the crowd. Some of them seemed outraged, especially when she had to nearly body-check the same tiny reporter she had collided with on the way out. She got Kellaway inside without any further trouble and let out a tremendous sigh of relief when the doors closed behind them.

"I'm so sorry," Kellaway said. "I had no idea it could be like that and…what the hell?"

"It's okay," Avery said. "You handled yourself well. They can be monsters if you let them. Don't be too hard on yourself. Just shake it off and refocus."

"Hey, Detective Black?"

Avery looked back to the officer that she had practically thrown Stefon Scott toward. He looked confused, securing a man who had just now started to get a hold of himself and stop crying.

"Sorry," Avery said. "Can you please get him to interrogation?"

The officer nodded and started down the hallway. Avery followed behind him, headed for Connelly's office. Kellaway went with her and they both found the office empty.

"Get on the phone and get Connelly and O'Malley," Avery said. "Let them know who we have and what he's done. Tell them I intend to start interrogation in fifteen minutes if they want to be here for it."

Kellaway did as she was asked but as she pulled up the first number, it was clear that she thought it was all a bit unorthodox. Avery supposed it was; she should certainly wait until everyone was present and accounted for before she started grilling Stefon. But she had come onto this case late and felt like she was making up for lost time.

She looked back toward the end of the hall where, through the glass doors, she could still see the media swarming like a nest of hornets. This case was just too good—too sweet for them not to be salivating over. Avery understood it and it made her start to wonder if the absurdity and graphic nature of the case was, in some way, behind the killer's motive.

With that thought in her head, she started down toward interrogation. She thought of the spiders in the glass case in Stefon's house and the way he had reacted to the mere insinuation that he had killed Lawnbrook. She let it all settle in her head as she gave O'Malley and Connelly time to join her.

Whether it was the thrill of the hunt or just the comfort of something familiar, Avery wasn't sure—but she found herself bouncing back and forth on the heels of her feet to get started. She wondered if she, too, was sort of like an angry hornet, swarming around its nest with its stinger primed and ready to bite.

***

Stefon was no longer crying when Avery joined him in the interrogation room. In the end, she'd made him wait for nearly an hour. It wasn't just to give O'Malley and Connelly a chance to arrive but to let Stefon stew in the events of the afternoon. She watched him through a monitor in the neighboring room, watching his expression go from thoughtful to sad, from pensive to worried.

Now, sitting across the table from him, Avery gave him a moment to get used to her being in the room. She'd easily bested him in conversation and physical ability at his house so he needed to be reminded of that by her silence. She knew that O'Malley, Connelly, and Kellaway were watching from the same spot she had been sitting less than five minutes ago. She thought of Kellaway and how she could best direct the interrogation so that the young officer might learn a thing or two.

65

"Do you have an account of everywhere you have been this week or week and a half?" Avery asked. Her tone was gentle and conversational, clearly not what Stefon had been expecting.

"I didn't do much of anything," he said. "I spent most of it at the house with Clarissa."

"And how long has she been staying with you?"

"Today makes three days that she's *stayed* there. But she's come over a few times before that."

"When was the earliest?" Avery asked.

"Three weeks ago, maybe?"

"Were you still physically involved with Alfred Lawnbrook at that time?"

"That's personal."

"Yes, I suppose it is. But since Alfred Lawnbrook is dead, I don't see how it can harm you or him. So…were you involved with Alfred when you started seeing Clarissa?"

"Not really," Stefon said, looking away in an ashamed manner. "I mean, we had hooked up a few days before I invited Clarissa to my house. But like I said…there was no relationship with Alfred. Just fooling around."

"And he knew this?"

"Yeah. We both wanted it that way."

"Before her stay of three days, when was the last time Clarissa had spent time with you?"

He thought about it for a moment before answering. "Two days before. We spent the day together. Had lunch, went back to my house and messed around. Had dinner. She left for her house around midnight."

"She indicated that you guys stay up late. What do you do during those late hours?"

"Hit up some parties. But…it's mainly just sex. She'll tell you the same. We're both…I don't know. Freaky, I guess."

"Freaky in the same way you thought Alfred got off on knowing there were spiders in the same room even though he was terrified of them?"

"Sort of."

"Well, we'll talk to Clarissa and check your alibis. If we can determine your whereabouts within twenty-four hours of Alfred Lawnbrook's death, you'll be free to go. It will have to be airtight, though. You have to understand how bad this looks for you, right?"

"Yeah," he said. "But I swear…it wasn't me. You know…even if you can't come up with an alibi between me and Clarissa, there

66

might be something on my computer. You guys can track log-ins and log-outs, right?"

"We can. Why do you ask?"

"The forum I met Clarissa on...I'm on there a lot. I've been trying to make some connection to maybe write articles for people. About spiders and things like that. Some obscure online nature mags pay pretty good for that kind of stuff."

Avery recalled seeing the beginnings of a few articles on his coffee table. It wasn't an alibi by any means, but it was at least something that added up.

"We'll look into that," Avery said. "In the meantime...can you remember anything Alfred ever said that might make you think he had enemies? Someone who really had it out for him?"

"No. He was a quiet dude. I mean, he was afraid of what his mom would think if she knew he was in a gay relationship but...no, nothing like enemies."

"And do you know of anyone else that knew of his intense fear of spiders?" Avery asked.

Again, Stefon put some actual thought into his answer before slowly shaking his head. "Not that I know of. He seemed to be embarrassed about it, though. So I guess he wouldn't really have shared it."

"And have you told anyone else about his fear?"

"I told Clarissa. But that was right after I saw that he had died. Me and her, we got in a fight about that. She said it would be a good way to go and I thought it was insensitive."

Avery nodded, relaxing a bit. She was pretty sure Stefon Scott had nothing to do with the murder of Alfred Lawnbrook. Even though the trail pointed there, it was all in his demeanor and his willingness to have them look into his computer records and speak to Clarissa.

"We're going to need you to stay here until your alibis are checked out," Avery said, getting to her feet. "In the meantime, I suggest you do your best to be polite to anyone else that asks you questions. Do you understand?"

He nodded, finding it hard to look at her. "You know," he said. "There's one thing about Alfred that I found a little weird...but it only just dawned on me right now."

"What's that?" she asked.

"He was open to the possibility of facing his fear of spiders. I think that's really the only reason he kept seeing me. He wanted to get over the fear. And I know I didn't kill him, even though you aren't convinced. But...if he wanted to get over a fear that badly, I

67

couldn't be the only one he told, right? Someone else *had* to have known. Someone he trusted."

It was a good point. Avery had considered it already but the way Stefon put it added a new twist.

He wanted to get over his fear of spiders.

She felt like it meant something, but she wasn't sure what just yet. But she thought Stefon was right: if he was set on overcoming his fear, he likely told more than one person. And if it had not been his mother, then who?

It was a good question…and one she thought they needed to find an answer to as soon as possible.

CHAPTER FIFTEEN

Abby Costello found her mind racing in some strange directions as her body was jostled and shaken. As a huge movie buff, she had seen far too many movies where someone is captured and put into the trunk of a car. She'd always thought that it was unrealistic—that a full-grown person could not bend in a way that would allow them to fit inside.

It was ironic, then, that she had found out just how wrong she had been. Only, *ironic* wasn't the word. *Horrifying* was a better word.

It was a fitting word, for sure. She was blindfolded and had something wrapped tightly around her mouth. She was pretty sure it was a ball gag. And she was indeed in a trunk. And with the exception of an ache in her knees where her legs were bent, it turned out that she had fit inside it easily enough.

She wasn't quite sure how she had gotten here. She'd been a little excited when her date had asked if she wanted to try something different. And when he had pulled out the straps and blindfold, her mind had gone two ways: one, excited and a little turned on; two, a very quiet and creeping unease.

Abby knew she was a good-looking woman. She'd known since high school when three guys had asked her to the prom, something that had been reinforced in college when not only one but two fights had erupted at frat parties over her. She'd never had problems getting a date or the attention of men. Therefore, she had always had full control of her sex life. She could have it when she wanted and was okay turning it down, knowing that it would come along again whenever she had the need.

She'd felt a slight need when she'd met her date that night. She knew she'd eventually sleep with him. He was cute and he treated her like a queen. But now she was gagged and blindfolded in his trunk. Now she was smelling the car's exhaust and something that smelled like dust and mothballs in the trunk.

It was even scarier when the car came to a stop. She figured he had been driving her around for about half an hour. She tried to roll over onto her back, hoping to somehow escape when he opened the trunk. But, as it happened, she could not manage to get off of her side. When he popped the trunk open a few seconds after killing the engine, she felt the cool air and would have given just about anything to see where they were.

She tried speaking to him, asking *Where are we and why are you doing this?* But all that came through the gag was a muffled noise.

She felt his hand grab her wrist, which was bound behind her back with the straps she had seen an hour ago and assumed would be tied to a headboard. He yanked her up easily but not with the gentle hands that she'd allowed to caress her breasts the few times they'd met before. He was rougher now and not at all interested in her most secret areas.

"We're here," he told her as he helped her to stand.

She felt the car's bumper against the back of her legs. Without her eyes, she could only use scent and sound to determine where they were. Neither of those senses helped much; the night was quiet and her nose was still cluttered with the smell of exhaust and the inside of his trunk.

"Come on," he said, his voice in her ear.

She tried pulling away, lunging hard to the right. He yanked her back, his grip like a vise now.

"Try that again and I'll break your arm," he said. His voice was calm and almost reasonable.

She began to sob through the gag, a sound that was like the mewling of a wounded animal. She was shaking as he led her forward. Three steps, then six, then ten, then twenty. She was pretty sure they were on grass and then hard-packed dirt.

And then she heard and felt wood beneath her feet. A few more steps and the wood seemed to shift slightly under her feet—almost like it was wobbling.

Then she heard the very light sounds of splashing—of water under the wood.

No, she tried to say, but it came out in a muffled whine against the gag.

Just thinking of water made her lungs ache. Blind panic seized her and she suddenly found it very hard to breathe.

God, no. Please...

She froze in place and fought against him again. Let him break her arm. She didn't care. She had to get away. Her blood was flooded with what felt like acid as terror spread its arms wide through her body.

A dock—I'm on a dock. There's water...a body of it. But where? Oh God...

70

Still, she fought to breathe. The fear was like some vise around her lungs. There was not a single drop of water on her, yet she felt like she was drowning.

He did not break her arm. Instead, he punched her hard in the back, right at the kidney. She buckled and fell and without giving her a moment to recover, he started dragging her forward. Her knees scraped against the wood—the wood of a dock or small pier, she assumed. Even as he dragged her, she could hear the water.

The water…waiting for her. Waiting to swallow her up into its deep and limitless belly. She shuddered and tried screaming through the gag. She wished he'd just kill her. Shoot her. Stab her. Bash her brains in…just please God, not the water.

Miraculously, he removed the blindfold in that moment. She saw that her other senses had done their job. She found herself on the edge of a small pier, looking out onto a body of water. Night had not yet fallen and the light of dusk on the water would have been beautiful…if it hadn't been for the water. That murky, deadly water.

As she looked at it, her bowels clenched and her lungs seemed to shudder. Her chest grew tight and she started to sob.

"I know you're scared," he said from behind her. "And that's okay. There's nothing wrong with being scared."

Abby could see street lights in the distance, probably having just clicked on. She wondered if she could make enough noise through the gag for anyone out that way to hear her. She wondered where they were. Where in the city was there this much water? It certainly wasn't the harbor. It was too pretty…too quiet.

Her thoughts were broken when she felt his hands snaking around her neck. She tried to fight away again and this time was rewarded with a hard knee to the small of her back. She crumpled again and this time when she hit her knees, she fell on the pier less than a foot away from the water. She gasped, her heart hammering in her chest and—

That's when his foot struck her backside. She went off the pier in a little half-flip. When she heard the splash and felt the water rushing past her head to swallow up her body, she tried to scream. But the gag would not let her and the pressure of the water made it impossible. She kicked her legs and tried to swim, realizing that her hands were still tied behind her back. She kicked and whimpered, knowing the surface was somewhere overhead. She could swim, knew *how to* swim, but the panic was too much.

She managed to break the water a single time. She saw her date, the man she thought had been cute and very kindhearted,

71

sitting on the dock and watching her. He smiled at her, his eyes fiery and intense.

His face was the last thing she saw. The panic and fear was simply too much.

When Abby went under the second time, she never made it back up.

CHAPTER SIXTEEN

By seven thirty that afternoon, Avery's hunch was proven to be true. Stefon had not one but two solid alibis for his whereabouts during the timeframe of Alfred Lawnbrook's murder. A series of video files that had been saved to his computer and heavily edited took up almost three days that—based on new information from the coroner—bookended the suspected time of Lawnbrook's death. The videos, of course, were about spiders and featured the three tarantula wolf spiders he'd had in the glass case in his living room.

The second alibi had come from Clarissa, who had happily handed her iPhone over to show a series of text messages from Stefon during that same time. And while the texts could have easily been sent from anywhere, it was the two long phone calls that proved most useful.

Stefon was released and went peacefully. Avery nearly felt the need to apologize to him but didn't bother. She wouldn't have done it three months ago and, quite honestly, wasn't sure why she felt the need to do so now. Maybe the three months off had softened her a bit. That or the emotional hell she'd been through over the course of those three months.

Stefon's release set Avery back to zero. She was only left with vague questions and theories, none of which had yet developed feet. She sat in her old office with Kellaway, Finley, and O'Malley. The space was cramped but Finley seemed to love the fact that his office was being used in such a way. Kellaway, meanwhile, seemed appreciative to be part of such a high-profile case. Still, she was keeping a cool ahead about her and was not holding a grudge toward Avery's little outburst earlier in the day.

Little by little, Avery was growing to like her quite a bit.

"What about drugs?" Kellaway asked as they tried their best to ping-pong ideas back and forth off of one another.

"What about them?" O'Malley asked.

"Were there any drugs in Lawnbrook's system?" she asked.

"Toxicology reports say no," O'Malley answered.

"But maybe there's an avenue there somewhere," Avery said. "Stefon claimed Lawnbrook was interested in getting over his fear of spiders. He also insinuated that having sex in the same room where there were spiders might have been an attempt to help with

73

the fear. I've also learned that there's apparently a small online community that is obsessed with spiders. It makes me wonder…if Lawnbrook was willing to confide his secret to Stefon and try any means necessary to overcome this fear, maybe he went elsewhere with it, too. Maybe he *did* know the killer. Maybe Lawnbrook met him online and the interaction with the spiders was intentional. Maybe it just got out of hand."

"It's certainly worth looking into," O'Malley said.

"Yeah, but that was a shitload of spiders," Finley said. "You'd think you'd sort of ease yourself into it if you're trying to get over a fear."

Avery nodded. It was a good point. Still, the thought of the exposure to the spiders being intentional had legs—especially if Stefon was accurate in just how badly Lawnbrook had wanted to get over his fear.

"What if it was Lawnbrook himself?" Kellaway suggested. "What if he had slowly collected them—either to get over his fear or to impress Stefon Scott?"

"Possible," O'Malley said. "Finley, can you get someone on that for us? Someone to nose around the Internet to find these weirdo communities. See if you can find any link to Lawnbrook."

"I'll sic a few people on it," Finley said, getting up from the desk.

"And I'm going to get back home," Avery said. "I'll do some digging of my own." She gave Kellaway a little nod of appreciation and then exited the office. She got perhaps five steps away before Kellaway's voice stopped her from behind.

"Detective Black?" Kellaway asked. "Um, can I ask a favor?"

"What is it?"

"My car broke down three days ago. I've been taking the bus to and from work and I was wondering if you could give me a ride?"

"Sure," Avery said, noting how embarrassed Kellaway seemed to be asking for the favor. "And hey," Avery added after some thought, "you can drop the Detective Black stuff. If we're going to work this case to completion, you can call me Avery."

This seemed to make Kellaway's day, as she was unable to contain her smile. Avery hid her own grin, finding some comfort in the fact that she could at least make *some* people happy.

***

"I feel like I need to apologize to you," Avery said. They were words that had never come to her very easily, not even when

74

interacting with Rose. But given the course of her life over the last three months, she figured there were some things she needed to change about herself.

"For what?" Kellaway said.

"For sort of snapping at you earlier when you were asking those questions about Howard Randall."

Kellaway considered it for a moment as she looked out of Avery's passenger side window. The apology seemed to surprise her, taking her off guard for a moment. Finally, she said, "You don't have anything to apologize for. I got overexcited. I mean…don't get me wrong. I saw some pro-level shit in New York, but the whole Howard Randall connection and all of your cases had me geeking out."

"I'm not geek-out worthy," Avery said. "Trust me."

"The stories I've heard about you say otherwise. It sort of blew me away that so many macho men were speaking so highly of you."

"Macho?" Avery asked with a chuckle. "Like who?"

Kellaway shrugged. "Most of them. I get it, you know. They're trying to put on a show, trying to seem tougher than they really are. I'm young and small-built. They're going to rib me and give me a hard time."

"Not too much of a hard time, I hope. Not a PR-reportable hard time."

"Oh, no…nothing like that."

"Most of the guys at the A1 are pussycats," Avery said. "You just need to assert yourself. And so far, it doesn't seem like that's an issue for you."

"It never has been," Kellaway said. "I'm actually more concerned about what you think of me, if I'm being honest."

"Don't be."

"Well…you got stuck with me on your first day back and I still don't really even know the full details about why you left."

Avery recognized this as a not-so-subtle way for Kellaway to ask about the last few months. Avery didn't mind. Surprisingly, she welcomed it. It would be good to speak to someone other than a therapist about it—especially someone who knew very little about her personal life.

"I left because everything seemed like it came falling down all at once," she said. "My ex-husband died, killed by a man I was trying to track down…all while my daughter was also being tormented. And then Ramirez died—and I don't know how much you know about him but…"

"You guys were involved, right?" Kellaway asked.

75

"Yeah. It was more serious than I admitted to myself. I didn't realize how much he meant to me until he was right there at the edge of death. He had a ring…was ready to get married."

Kellaway nodded solemnly, perhaps feeling that she had opened a door she wasn't ready to step through just yet. "Well," she said quietly, "how is your daughter doing after all of it? At least you still have her."

Avery tried to muster up a fake laugh but couldn't manage it. "You'd think. But…no. Rose is more distant than ever. She blames me for her dad's death. And she claims my career has always kept her in harm's way. And the hell of it is that she might be right."

It was strange to talk to Kellaway about Rose. After all, Kellaway might be five or six years older than Rose…it was far too close to speaking to Rose herself.

"So…if you don't mind me asking, what made you come back?" Kellaway asked.

Avery knew the answer. It was an easy one but that made it somehow harder to answer. "Because it's the only thing that makes sense to me," she said. "I tried to tell myself that I didn't miss it, but I did. It's all I know. And really, I think Ramirez would be disappointed in me if I didn't carry on."

Somehow, the conversation had sped the strip along. Avery took the final turn as directed by Kellaway. It brought them to a nice apartment complex about twenty minutes away from the precinct. Kellaway paused a moment before opening the door. She looked back to Avery thoughtfully.

"You know…I know it's not the same," she told Avery, "but my folks divorced when I was twelve. Then my father died in a car accident when I was fifteen. I hated my mother. If I'm being honest, I still haven't fully forgiven her. But I have reached out, especially now that she's not well. I've talked to her and she's not completely shut out anymore. So, the thing with your daughter…give it time. She'll come around."

"That's the hope," Avery said…without much hope at all.

Kellaway stepped out and closed the door. Avery watched her go, trying her best not to let the unexpected conversation pull her toward grief. She pulled away before it had a chance to sink its claws in, though her thoughts remained very close to Rose.

Give it time. She'll come around.

It was a pleasant thought, a bit of encouragement wrapped up nice with a little bow on top. But Avery seriously doubted that it was true.

76

CHAPTER SEVENTEEN

Avery spent a portion of that night in front of her laptop. She was trying to determine the types of places someone might order a funnel web spider. There were an alarming number of places, a few of which seemed highly illegal yet given a very professional façade. She then allowed herself to slip down a bit of a rabbit hole in doing more digging on Stefon Scott—not because she believed him to be a suspect but because he seemed to have been something of a central character in the little online communities he had talked about.

She read a few of his posts from one of the arachnid-centric forums, getting his user information from an article that had been linked to a bio page on the Boston Science Museum's website—a bio that she was sure had not yet been removed solely because someone had not thought to take it down. She also discovered on those forums that acquiring venomous spiders that were not considered "local" was often considered illegal and immoral.

As she looked back over Lawnbrook's case files, something peculiar struck her for the first time. Whoever had brought those spiders to Lawnbrook's apartment had not bothered trying to collect them up afterward. If the person had been a spider enthusiast, it seemed unlikely that they would just leave the spiders there. On top of that was the fact that Stefon claimed Lawnbrook wanted to get over his fear.

So maybe the spiders aren't the central focus here, she thought. *Maybe his fear is where the case needs to be explored from. Maybe his fear was the motive...*

It seemed flimsy but certainly worth some thought.

Only, it was harder to think about than she cared to admit. Truthfully, ever since her conversation with Kellaway, Avery's attention had mostly been turned toward Rose. It's why she had such a hard time connecting with anything she read on the forums or in Lawnbrook's case files.

She checked her phone and saw that it had somehow already gotten to be 9:20. She was pretty sure Rose was at work, getting some of those amazing tips she had boasted about. Still, Avery tried to give her a call. It rang once before going straight to voicemail. Avery toyed with the idea of sending a text but ultimately decided against it. She figured it would have to be Rose's decision if there was to be any repair. Rose would have to make the next move.

But her personal life had never been too different from her career; Avery was not one to rely on patience to help resolve problems. She knew Rose was a master at the silent treatment and worried just how long she'd be able to hold up.

"Shit," Avery said into the empty cabin.

She slid her phone away from her and shut her laptop down. For her first day back on the job, it had been an exhausting one. She couldn't remember the last time she had gone to bed before eleven, but it was happening tonight. Alternatively, she could not remember the last time she had set her cell phone on her bedside table when going to bed—but that was happening for the first time in three months as well.

She was working again...on the clock again. And while there was a certain amount of pressure and weight to that fact, it also helped her to fall asleep faster than she had since Ramirez had died. Now, instead of focusing on what she had done wrong during the case that had resulted in his death, she was able to instead focus on the things she could do right on her current case.

***

There were spiders crawling up her arms. One had reached her shoulder and was scurrying its way to the curve of her neck. She opened her mouth to scream and another one—a spider the size of a quarter—came leaping off of her tongue.

It was this one coming out of her mouth that clued Avery's subconscious brain into the fact that this was nothing more than a bad dream. A *very* bad dream.

The spiders were coming from everywhere—from webs on the ceiling, from under the bed, from within her hair, from under her clothes. She shot up in bed, realizing that she wasn't in bed at all but on one of those metal slabs in the morgue. Alfred Lawnbrook was lying beside her. He was dead yet his head lolled back and forth. When he looked over in her direction, he smiled. Numerous tiny spiders came skittering out from between his teeth.

He then spoke. When he did, it sounded like a drawbridge opening. "Who are you, Avery?" he asked, miming Howard Randall's letter.

He opened his mouth and she watched as an enormous spider leg came inching out. Lawnbrook made a retching noise as the leg came out of his mouth. It was huge and hairy, easily the size of a

78

large lobster's claw. The body attached to it, along with the other legs, started to show in the back of his mouth, glistening and tight.

The dream shattered with that absurdity and Avery sat up quickly in bed—in her real bed this time. No metal slab, no smiling corpse beside her.

She gasped, unaware that she was brushing at her arms and shoulder to rid herself of the phantom spiders. She slid out of bed, feeling that they were in the covers. She caught her breath and walked to the bathroom for a glass of water.

That's when she realized that the dream itself had not stirred her awake. It had been the buzzing of her phone. She had purposefully left it by her bedside in the chance that she got a call at night but the habits of the last three months had caused her to turn the ringer off when she had gotten ready for bed.

She ran to it and picked it up with hands that still felt as if there were spiders crawling on them. She saw Finley's name on the screen, as well as the time in the top right corner: 3:07 in the morning.

"Hey, Finley," she said.

"Welcome back to work," he said. "Don't you miss the late hours?"

"What's up?" she asked.

"We found a body," he said. "Pretty sure it's not related to Lawnbrook but still sort of creepy all the same. You want in on it?"

She considered for only a moment before responding. "What's the address?"

CHAPTER EIGHTEEN

The searchlights bordering the small cove along the western edge of Jamaica Pond looked like something out of a sci-fi film from a distance—like several UFOs had come down to the body of water, waiting to kick off an invasion. There were a few police vehicles parked fifty or so feet away from the water and a few people scattered around the scene.

Avery parked behind a police cruiser and found Finley right away. He was standing over near the water, next to a small pier that extended out into the pond for a distance of about twenty feet. The pier looked very rickety, the sort of thing that had been well used several years ago and then neglected and abandoned.

Finley and three other officers were huddled around a body that had been laid down on a plastic tarp. It was a woman of about twenty or so—far too close to Rose's age as far as Avery was concerned. Her hands were bound behind her back and there was something around her neck, a cloth of some kind.

"Any ID yet?" Avery asked.

"Not yet, but we'll have it soon," Finley said. "There was a debit card tucked into her back pocket. We've got the info being run right now. Should be any minute."

Avery knelt down by the body for a closer look. The searchlights were some help, but Finley assisted in aiming a small flashlight at the body. Avery looked her over, doing everything she could to push images of Rose out of her mind.

The girl was quite pretty and surely weighed no more than one hundred and ten pounds. She had blonde hair that was a bit longer than shoulder-length and her blue eyes were wide open, staring up into the night sky. She was fully dressed, wearing a white long-sleeved top and a pair of tight-fitting jeans. Her hands had been bound with basic cord, a thick rope that had been expertly tied. The cloth around her neck was tied in the same type of knot, but it was loose-fitting. It had not been used to strangle her but looked dangerous nonetheless.

"This cloth on her neck," Avery said. "I put my money on it being used as a blindfold. Her killer didn't want her to know where they were going."

80

"I don't see any visible bruising," Finley said. "No scratches or abrasions. No signs of a struggle from what I can see and—"

Another officer approached, walking quickly from the direction of the parked cruisers. "I got an ID from that debit card," he said. "The victim is Abby Costello. Twenty-two years old, an employee at an accounting firm here in Boston."

"Did you get an address?" Avery asked.

"Yes. We've got three officers headed over that way as we speak," the cop said.

Finley looked down at Avery with a playfully suspicious look. "What are you thinking?" he asked.

"Her eyes," Avery said. "They're wide open. She was scared when she died, I think. Very scared."

"Well, yeah. What's so crazy about that?"

"Nothing at first glance. But if she was killed prior to being dumped, I don't think there would be this expression of horror on her face. Besides…I see no indication of foul play before she was dumped into the water."

"So you think the killer blindfolded her, brought her out to this random-ass pier, tied her hands behind her back, and tossed her in the water?"

"Yeah. I think the cause of death is going to be drowning. Her body wasn't just dumped in an attempt to get rid of it."

"Well, the ambulance is on its way," Finley said. "The coroner should be able to verify that pretty quickly, I'd think."

Avery stood up and walked out onto the pier. On its face, Abby Costello's death bore no similarities to Alfred Lawnbrook's. Still, the concept would not leave her alone. Maybe she still had spiders on the brain from that jarring nightmare…but she felt like there had to be some sort of connection.

Or maybe you're trying to make one already messed up case much bigger than it is, she thought. *Maybe you want that sort of trophy case in front of you after being gone for three months.*

"Who discovered the body?" she asked.

"A guy out walking his dog," Finley said. "Or so he said. When the first officers on the scene arrived, they said they smelled pot on his breath. The guy said he saw what looked like a lump of weird weeds floating out there. Hard to tell because it was so dark. As he got closer to the pier, he saw that it wasn't weeds but blonde hair."

"How long has the body been out of the water?" Avery asked.

"Forty minutes. She'd only been out for five or ten minutes before I called you."

Avery looked around at the scene. She knew that there were sections of Jamaica Pond that often drew sizeable crowds, especially on the weekend. But this little cove was off the beaten path, the sort of place teens came to make out or smoke pot. The chance of finding a witness to what happened was slim to none.

"Was the debit card the only thing on her?" Avery asked.

"Yeah," Finley said. "No cash, no phone…which I found strange. A girl this pretty at this stage of life…they're supposed to be glued to their phones, right?"

"The killer probably took it," Avery said. "That or it's somewhere at the bottom of the pond."

She looked at Abby Costello again, trying to determine how long her body had been in the water. Her clothes were soaked and her hair was matted. Avery hunkered down next to the body again and saw that Abby's fingers were covered in wrinkles that often came from sitting in a tub of water for too long—only Abby's were *very* wrinkled. Her palms had also gone a hard shade of white.

"I'd estimate that she was in the water for at least two hours," Avery said. "Maybe the coroner can tell us more. Given that span of time, I doubt it would do good to make a perimeter of the area. We'll hope we can get some fingerprints from her body or the blindfold."

In the distance, she could see the ambulance lights. She once again looked back out to the water, wondering what secrets it might be hiding.

***

Within another fifteen minutes, the officers who had been dispatched to Abby's apartment called back. They'd broken the news to her roommate, another woman in her early twenties. She was distraught by the news and the only bit of information she could offer was that Abby had gone out on a date that evening. She didn't know the guy's name, as Abby tended to be very reserved and quiet about her love life.

When the police had searched Abby's room, they'd discovered a box from an online retailer. The box had been open and inside was a brand new smartphone. The phone had been powered up but not yet set up or programmed. The package receipt inside gave an order date of two days ago. A quick call to the delivery service confirmed that the phone had arrived earlier in the day—maybe a few hours before Abby Costello had been tossed into Jamaica Pond.

It was this bit of information that Avery, Kellaway, and Finley were discussing in an A1 conference room twenty minutes after Abby's body had been removed from the scene. It was 4:30 in the morning, the coffee was brewing, and Avery's day was just getting started.

"This could maybe actually work out in our favor," Avery said, pouring a cup of coffee.

"Having no phone at all?" Finley asked. "How's that?"

"Because if she has a brand new phone, it means that her contract for her old one was probably up. That or it was just crapping out on her. How many times in the past when you have upgraded your phone did you simply just throw the old one in the trash?"

"Never," Kellaway said. "I usually keep mine as a backup music player."

"And when Rose was younger," Avery said, "I'd keep my old ones for her to play games on. But either way...if Abby Costello had just received a new phone, the old one is probably still around somewhere and not at the bottom of the pond, as I had feared."

"The cops at her apartment never found the old one, though," Finley pointed out.

"So then we contact her service provider," Avery said. "If they can't get us the physical phone itself, they probably have records of phone calls and texts that we can use to find the killer."

"There are those ecoATMs, too," Kellaway said. "Those little things that look like miniature recycling bins where you can get rid of your old phone. It's like a recycling initiative or something."

"Great point," Avery said. "We'll need to assign someone to all of these tasks as soon as the local mobile and wireless stores open up."

"So what do we do in the meantime?" Finley asked.

"You do whatever O'Malley and Connelly have you doing around here," Avery said with a bit of pride in her voice. The smile he gave her warmed her heart. "As for Kellaway and I, we'll start talking to the roommate and the family. And please, if you don't mind, direct the calls from the coroner to me as they come in."

"Aren't you more worried about the spider case?" Finley asked.

"I am," she said. "But I have a hunch..."

"That they're connected?" Finley asked. "Really?"

"I'm going to assume they are until it can be proven otherwise."

Finley shrugged and got up for his own cup of coffee. "Hey…if you want to overwork yourself within your first two days back, be my guest. Either way…it's good to have you back."

She said nothing to this, mainly because she wasn't sure if she was really, truly *back*. It felt like it, but that could just be the excitement of it all. Whatever the feeling was, it was thrumming through her as she and Kellaway left the conference room, heading out into the early morning with two murders to solve.

CHAPTER NINETEEN

Abby Costello's roommate was a sobbing mess when Avery and Kellaway arrived at their apartment. She was another petite blonde, barely able to keep herself in a sitting position on the couch when they arrived. Her name was Amy Dupree and even before Avery had the chance to question her, there was quite a bit that she surmised about the two girls simply based on the apartment.

The pictures of Abby and Amy in the living room showed them cheesing in front of a camera with parties going on behind them. One of the picture frames bore the Greek letters that made up Sigma Sigma Sigma—Tri Sig.

Sorority sisters from college, Avery thought. It at least helped her better understand why Amy was taking the news of Abby's death so particularly hard.

Maybe it was because of the age similarities between them, but Kellaway managed to take the lead in getting Amy to calm down long enough to answer a few basic questions. Amy still sobbed and sniffled through the questions but she was at least finally able to form some coherent sentences.

"You told the first officers that came by that Abby had a date tonight," Kellaway said. "But you didn't know the guy's name…that Abby kept her love life to herself. Is that right?"

"Yeah. She was always like that. Abby wasn't a relationship sort of girl, you know? She'd see a guy for a few weeks, maybe a few months depending on the guy, and then it would just sort of end. She had one serious relationship in college that ended with him cheating on her. There was a pregnancy scare in there, too. And ever since then, she's been very private about the guys she sees."

"Did she say anything at all about this date tonight?" Avery asked.

"No. She never told me his name, what he looked like…nothing like that. Just that he was cute and a little older."

"Do you know how much older?"

"I'd guess maybe no older than forty. Abby had this funny thing for older guys, but swore she'd never get involved with anyone over forty."

"Any idea how long she'd been seeing him?"

"Maybe two or three weeks. If that. I really couldn't tell you."

85

"And what about the new phone she ordered?" Avery asked. "Do you know why she ordered it?"

"Yeah, the old one had a crack in the screen. It still worked fine, but the crack annoyed her. She called up the company and had it replaced."

"Do you know what she did with the old one?" Avery asked.

"No idea."

Avery looked around at all of the pictures again. The two smiling blonde girls looking out at her from those pictures looked like something out of a storybook.

"What about Jamaica Pond?" Avery asked. "Do you know if she had any ties to the location? Or had you ever heard her mention it?"

"God no," Amy said sternly, almost on the verge of breaking into deep sobs again. "That was maybe the worst part about hearing she had died...*how* she had died. Abby was scared of water. I mean, she'd get in a pool as long as there was a shallow end. But open bodies of water scared the hell out of her."

"Do you know why?" Avery asked.

"She almost drowned when she was a kid. Like ten or so, I think. Her family went to some lakefront property in Virginia. She was trying to learn to water-ski and there was some sort of freak thing with the rope. She went under for a while and the lifejacket she was wearing was too loose. Her head got trapped in it and it popped right off of her, I think. So yeah...she stayed away from water. We went to the beach for our senior year of college, us and about five friends. She never got in the ocean—always sat up on the sand, as far away as she could without being rude."

"So if her date had suggested they go for a moonlight stroll around Jamaica Pond, she wouldn't have gone for it?" Kellaway asked.

"Highly doubtful," Amy said.

Avery considered it for a moment and then headed for the door. "Amy, thank you so much for your time and help. If you happen to think of anything else that might assist us, please call us."

"Do you have anyone to be with you for the next day or so?" Kellaway asked.

Amy nodded. "My brother is coming over. He should be here in an hour or so. But I'm good...I'll be okay until he gets here."

Avery hated to leave a grieving woman alone, but she had more stops to make before the night was over. She and Kellaway made it out the door, closing it behind them, and then to the stairs before they heard the muffled sounds of Amy Dupree's crying.

86

"The water," Kellaway said as they got into the car. "It's like the spiders, isn't it?"

"You mean her fear of the water? Yes…it could be. But we can't jump to conclusions. There's a lot more information out there to be found."

It was a bullshit answer, just something to tell Kellaway that would help her to stay level and grounded. Because as far as Avery was concerned, two back-to-back cases where a victim's fear was used as the means of death pointed to a pretty clear intent on the killer's part. But she knew she needed more to go on before she could present her theory to the guys back at the A1.

So that's what she struck out to find as she pulled the car out into early morning traffic. It wasn't quite six o'clock yet and she was already on her way to speak to her second grieving individual of the day.

***

Abby Costello's mother lived in Virginia, ironically in the lakeside town where Abby had nearly drowned as a kid. Her father, however, lived with his second wife in the South End of Boston. By the time Avery and Kellaway arrived, Larry Costello had already been informed of his daughter's death by the same cops who had initially visited Amy.

Larry Costello stood behind his kitchen bar as Avery and Kellaway did their best to conduct a rational line of questioning. Larry was grieving in his own way: doing the dishes, scrubbing the counters, busying himself with throwing something together for breakfast. He wept the entire time he did these things but managed to give coherent answers to most of the questions.

"I hate to say it," Larry said, "but Amy is right. Abby was never one to tell me much about the guys she was dating. She did a bit in high school but that was just because of proms and curfews and things like that."

"Do you think she would have shared any information about this man with her mother?" Avery asked.

"I doubt it. They had a very strained relationship. They spoke on the phone maybe once a month and only saw one another around the holidays. It's a mutual I-don't-give-a-damn sort of relationship between both of them. God…someone has to tell her. I have to call her, don't I?"

"You can have someone on the police force do it if you like," Avery said.

87

"No. I'll do it," Larry said. "She'll handle it better coming from me. I…when can I see her? The body, I mean?"

He let out a strangled moan of despair at the mention of *the body* but it passed quickly and he was right back to cracking a few eggs into a bowl. His wife poked her head out of the bedroom when she heard the sound, saw that things were okay, and then headed back into the room.

"She's taking it hard," Larry said. "She and Abby had started to become friends. It took a while for Abby to warm up to her, but it was finally starting to feel natural. Anyway…can I see her?"

"You can," Avery said. "Of course, there's the autopsy to be conducted, but after that you can visit. Someone will contact you about   it."

"Is there anything else about your daughter you can tell us that might help with the case?" Kellaway asked.

"No. It might sound like the typical naïve father, but I don't know of any problems or bad behavior. I do agree with what Amy told you, though: Abby hated water. Was absolutely terrified of big open bodies of water. I can't believe she had to endure that. I suppose Amy probably told you about the near-drowning incident?"

"She did," Avery said.

Her cell phone rang at that moment. She grabbed it right away, hoping it was the coroner. She gave Kellaway a look, trying to indicate that the questioning was on her shoulders now.

"Sorry, I have to take this," Avery said, excusing herself into the Larry's living room. She answered the call on the fourth ring, trying to keep her voice down.

"This is Detective Black."

"Hi, Detective Black, this is Cho Yin from the coroner's office. I was told to contact you directly with the results on Abby Costello."

"Yes. What's the word?"

"She definitely drowned. Preliminary results show no signs of abuse or sexual activity. Of course, we'd rule it as murder, as her hands were bound behind her back."

"Yes. Definitely not a suicide. The blindfold proves that, I think."

"There is one more thing I thought you might find interesting," Yin said. "If you recall, when you and I discussed the Lawnbrook case, I pointed out that there had been extremely high levels of cortisol at the time of death, due to the fear."

"Yes, I remember."

"I found similarly high levels in Abby Costello. They weren't quiet as high as Lawnbrook's but she was certainly scared."

"Of course she was," Avery said. "She was blindfolded and led down a pier to the water."

Of course, now that she knew Abby had been afraid of water, she was looking for such a link. She was simply arguing the facts with Yin in order to get a second party to verify her gut reaction.

"Yes, but the levels I'm showing are higher than the expected levels we find in people who have been in situations where they were hunted down or pursued. Abby's fear was something not typical in other murder cases."

"So you'd say it was safe to say that she was scared of...what, the water?"

"Possibly," Yin said.

"Thanks for the call," Avery said. "Please let me know if you find anything else out of the ordinary."

With that, she pocketed the phone and went back into the kitchen. Kellaway was still talking to Larry, asking him about any college boyfriends Abby might have had. He was telling her that he knew there were a few but nothing serious. He never met them or knew their names.

"Mr. Costello, that was the coroner that just called. I believe they're done with the preliminary autopsy. You can go see her now if you like."

Larry nodded, stopping as he added cheese to the eggs that he had dumped into a frying pan on his stove. He then paused, still with shredded cheese in his hand, and lost it. His face crumpled in a way that hurt Avery to witness, and he hit his knees in the kitchen. He let out another wail and this time his wife came running out to his side. She'd kept away while they'd questioned him but this was just too much.

Avery and Kellaway stepped back, slowing them their privacy. She did not want to leave without formally saying goodbye, especially not when he was in the throes of his grief. So they walked into the living room while a grieving father mourned the loss of his daughter.

It then hit Avery like a brick, standing in the living room and listening to Larry Costello's sorrow.

This is why I do it, she thought. *This is why I've always done it and this is why I came back. To right the wrongs that cause this kind of pain. To catch the killers that take life away, robbing not just the victims, but the lives of their loved ones as well.*

89

And with that in mind, Avery knew that she would catch this killer. She felt the certainty in her bones, like fire burning her from the inside.

CHAPTER TWENTY

Never one to wait passively around while waiting for others to come up with answers, Avery headed back to the precinct. She had already formulated a plan of attack in her head, most of it requiring good old nose-to-the-grindstone research and digging. She figured she could do that while she waited for results from forensics and a final report from the coroner.

Without a proper office to call her own, she borrowed a laptop from the PR department and set up shop in one of the smaller conference rooms. Kellaway joined her and together, with coffee and donuts fueling them, they started working together like a well-oiled machine. Avery found that Kellaway took instruction well and never argued. She was legitimately happy to help in any way she could, even when it was to run basic records requests or doing simple Google searches.

The first thing they did was run database searches on Alfred Lawnbrook and Abby Costello. Aside from two speeding tickets on Alfred's end, they both came back clean. Kellaway then called Amy Dupree and asked about any hobbies or interests Abby enjoyed. The only answer was cooking and reading—neither avenue providing much in the way of research.

The trail didn't really start producing results until Avery decided to make a call to Phyllis Lawnbrook. She answered almost right away, still sounding worn out on the other end. After introductions and apologizing for dragging the pain of the case on, Avery got to a question she was starting to feel was important.

"Mrs. Lawnbrook, I wonder if you might remember what started Alfred's severe fear of spiders. Was there maybe some childhood incident that scarred him in some way?"

"Not that I can remember," she said. "I think it was just one of those natural things, you know? I always assumed he got it from his father...his father was deathly afraid of praying mantises. Even as a grown man, he'd leap back like a frightened child if he ever came across one."

"Do you recall the age when Alfred might have first started expressing a fear of spiders?" Avery asked.

"I don't know for sure. Maybe eight or so? It might have been as old as ten, but I'm not exactly sure about that."

Avery thanked her and ended the call, looking thoughtfully into her cup of coffee.

"You latch onto an idea?" Kellaway asked.

"Not an idea, exactly. Just…a thought. We know for a fact that Lawnbrook was at least working towards getting over his fear of spiders. And he went to some pretty extreme measures to get it done. And we also know that while Abby Costello was terrified of open bodies of water, she'd at least get into the shallow end of a pool. I don't know if that constitutes facing your fear or not. But…if these cases are linked—and I'm inclined to think they are—I'd be interested to see why their fears made them targets. I was hoping that if I could find out where the fears originated from, there could be pay dirt."

"But Abby's fear came from a freak water-skiing accident. How could anyone even know about that?"

"It's a good point. Still…it makes me wonder if there is anything that might link them? Why did the killer select *them*?"

"So you think it might be worth finding out if Alfred Lawnbrook and Abby Costello knew one another?"

"Exactly," Avery said, pulling out her phone again.

She called Larry Costello first. The phone was answered by his wife, who claimed that Larry had been a blubbering mess for most of the morning. Avery asked if it would be okay if she sent them a picture of someone to see if Larry recognized the face. After getting permission from the wife, Avery texted a picture of Alfred Lawnbrook, the candid picture that had been used in most newspapers over the last few days.

"Another thought for you," Kellaway said. "Amy said that Abby never really settled down. But she dated guys quite often. It makes me think there was a lot of dinners out for her. And if guys took her out to eat pretty often, she had to have a favorite place, right?"

"Right," Avery said, impressed with the logic behind the idea. "So if we can find a place that she frequented, maybe someone would have seen her last night—with her date."

"I'm on it," Kellaway said, pulling up Amy Dupree's number one more time.

Avery listened to Kellaway's end of the conversation, restraining herself from interjecting. It was nice to watch Kellaway at work; she had a way of communicating with people that didn't make them feel pressured or uneasy.

While she listened to the conversation, she received a text on her phone. It was from Larry Costello (or his wife). It read: *I don't know this guy. Should I?*

Avery replied back with a no, thanking them again for their help.

Less than a minute later, Kellaway ended her call. Avery could tell by the look on her face that Kellaway was getting excited. The thrill of the hunt had pretty much the same look whether on the face of a rookie or a seasoned pro.

"Mudslide Grill," Kellaway said. "According to Amy it was not only one of their favorite places during college, but it remained one of Abby's go-to places. She'd even use it as a scale to see if a guy was worth dating or not—whether or not the guy liked the food. And get this...Amy is pretty sure Abby had requested her date take her there last night."

Without another word, they both got up from the conference room table. As they hurried down the hallway and out into the parking lot, Avery was a bit ashamed that she had even considered the idea of using deer hunting as a lame substitute for the thrill that was currently racing through her.

***

It was barely ten o'clock in the morning when they pulled into the empty lot in front of Mudslide Grill. The hours of operation on the door read *10:30 – Midnight*. Avery tapped on the door, attracting the attention of the hostess who was helping to set the place up for the day's business. The hostess rolled her eyes and pointed to a nonexistent watch on her wrist. Avery tapped the glass again, this time showing her badge and giving her eyes their own little roll.

The hostess hurried over and unlocked the door. "I'm sorry," she said. "I had no idea you were a cop. We get some weird people that try to get in here early for those morning drinks. It's a little sad."

"It's okay," Avery said. "How many people are here with you right now?"

"Just three others. Two first-shift waitresses and my manager."

"Could you please gather them up for me and meet me at the bar area? I have a few really quick questions I need to ask about a woman that we think might have been here early last night."

93

"Sure thing," the hostess said. She took off toward the back of the restaurant quickly, excited to be in the center of what could potentially be some juicy drama and gossip.

Avery and Kellaway entered the bar area, freshly cleaned from the night before. Yet it still held the smell of spilled beer and stale over-sprayed cologne. A sign over the bar boasted that the place offered the best Mudslides in the country—apparently where the name of the place came from.

The hostess and the other three employees all arrived together. Avery could spot the manager right away; he was the upright-looking thirty-something leading the pack. There was worry and panic on his face whereas the expressions of the others—two women in their twenties and a male who looked fresh out of high school—were ones of excitement and curiosity.

"Are you the manager?" Avery asked the thirty-something leading the little pack. The name tag on his shirt read DAN.

"I am. What's this about?"

Avery showed him her badge and then pulled out her phone. "We're trying to determine if a certain woman was in here last night. Her name is Abby Costello and we have a fairly solid lead that makes us think she would have been here. Were any of you here last night after six in the evening?"

The hostess and the young-looking guy both raised their hands. "I was here until closing," the hostess said. Avery saw that her nametag read BRITTANY.

"I clocked out at ten," the young man said. His nametag read DEMARIUS.

Avery pulled up a picture of Abby that she had found on Facebook. The photo had been uploaded just three days ago, so it was very recent. "I know you see a lot of people in here every day," Avery said. "But if you could really try to remember this woman, I'd appreciate it."

"Oh, that's easy," Brittany said. "Yeah, I saw her. She was really nice. Very chatty."

"And was she on a date? Was there a man with her?"

"I think so," Brittany said. "I served them at the bar. The guy was sort of all over the place. He sat next to her but not for the whole time."

"And do you know what time this might have been?" Kellaway asked.

"Well, I remember them so well because it was pretty early—before it gets really busy for the dinner and drinking rush. I'd guess they were here around five thirty or so."

94

Avery then looked to Dan, the manager. "If I give you a debit card number, could you look through the evening's transactions to find out when it was used?"

"Yeah, I can do that."

"Kellaway, can you pull the card number from the files and set him to it?"

Kellaway nodded right away, thumbing through her phone with expert proficiency. She and Dan headed over to the register behind the bar.

"Brittany, this is very important...do you think you could identify the man she was with? Can you describe him?"

"He was tall. Maybe right at six feet...maybe a little over. Dark hair, good-looking in an unshaven sort of way. He was very intense, just the way he talked to people, you know? He was flirty with me when I served him but not in a gross way."

"And how did the woman seem to you? In a good mood? Something bothering her?"

"She seemed uptight at first, when the guy was with her. I caught her rolling her eyes a lot, like wishing he'd go away. That kind of thing."

"You said *when the guy was with her*. Was he not here with her the entire time?"

"No. I missed what happened but the guy left after a while. When he was gone, I saw the woman looking around nervously. I'm pretty sure she asked the woman beside her if she could use her phone at some point. I remember that because I thought it was weird that she didn't have a phone. *Everyone* has a phone, you know?"

"Did anyone else come in to meet her after her date left?"

"No. Not that I saw. I'm sorry...that's when it started to pick up. I barely remember her paying her check. I felt sort of sorry for her. I got the feeling that her date bailed on her."

"Do you know how long she was here *after* her date left?"

"No idea. Maybe half an hour."

From behind the bar, Kellaway called out. "Got it. Abby Costello paid her tab at six thirty-two yesterday afternoon. Two drinks, one shot, and a burger."

Avery considered the time for a moment and then added: "Brittany, do you remember Abby and this man maybe having harsh words at the bar?"

"No. Like I said, though...it was clear that she was annoyed about something."

Avery nodded, her head putting the scenario together. *So maybe they had an argument and the guy left...but then abducted her afterwards. Or, if Abby wasn't into serious relationships like Amy claims, maybe she met up with someone after the guy left. Maybe her date here last night is not the killer. But if it is...we at least need to check it somehow.*

She opened her mouth to start asking about the date that had left Abby, but her phone rang before she got the chance. She nearly ignored it but then thought it might be the coroner with some other interesting finding from Abby's autopsy.

When she saw that the number was one she didn't recognize, she nearly ignored it. But it was at that moment where something more than gut instinct kicked in. She'd experienced it maybe three times in her career, the urge to act one way or another based on nothing more than sheer feeling. It was almost supernatural in the way it washed through her. She knew she needed to answer the phone.

So she did.

"One moment," she said to the gathered Mudslide Grill employees. She turned her back to them and answered the call. "Avery Black," she said.

"Mrs. Black...this is Janell Mitchell calling with Boston Rescue and Emergency Services. I'm calling because I just got a call from one of our ambulance drivers stating that they are on the way to the hospital with your daughter."

Avery felt the world freeze all around her. Her mind seemed to refuse to accept the words she had just heard. "I'm sorry," she said. "You said my *daughter?*"

"Yes ma'am. Rose Black. She should be coming into the ER within the next five to seven minutes."

"I don't understand...what the hell happened?"

"We don't have full details yet, ma'am. But the driver and the medical attending to her seem to believe that it was a suicide attempt."

"A...*what?*"

The woman on the other end responded, repeating suicide attempt again, but Avery barely heard her. She was already running to the doors of Mudslide Grill in a half stumble. When she called over her shoulder to let Kellaway know what was happening, she was hardly aware of it. She felt like she was floating outside of herself, watching it unfold from some haunted place outside of this world.

96

When she pulled the car out of the lot, she saw Kellaway at the door but didn't acknowledge her. She had already started to cry and in some very dark place within her heart, wondered how she might herself commit suicide if she lost her daughter.

CHAPTER TWENTY ONE

Avery felt like she was drunk. That was how beyond her senses she was as she parked her car in the lot of the ER. Her legs felt wobbly and her stomach was a tumultuous pit that made her feel like she might puke at any moment. She ran into the ER waiting room, running so quickly that she nearly collided with the glass window that separated the receptionist desk from the waiting room area. She got Rose's check-in information and after showing her badge to one of the women behind the glass, was escorted as far into the emergency room as she was allowed to go.

When the woman stopped her before they reached the exam rooms, Avery nearly exploded. "No," Avery said. "No...I need to see her and I need to see her now!"

"Ma'am, I understand your distress but even though you have that badge, there are certain rules we just can't break. I've already paged to have the doctor come and speak with you and for now that's just the best I can do."

"Well, it's not enough!"

The woman nodded. "I know. It's not. But...those are the rules. You're a cop...surely you understand the need for rules, right?"

It was an elementary tactic, but it worked. It also helped that as she stood at the intersection of four different hallways with the woman, she saw a doctor hurriedly approaching from the left. The woman who had escorted her saw the doctor coming, waved, and took her leave—probably glad to be rid of the panicked and bossy detective.

"Are you Ms. Black?" the doctor asked.

"I am. How's Rose?"

He sighed and his eyes focused intently on her. *My God,* Avery thought. *She's dead. It's too late. I've lost her...*

"It's too early to tell right now," the doctor said. "However, if I had to make a bet—which I never would, by the way—I think she's going to be okay."

"And it was a suicide attempt?" Avery asked, still unable to believe it. "They're sure of this?"

"Yes. And once we get the tests back, I'm pretty sure that will confirm it. She overdosed on Oxycontin. We don't know how much she took, but the pill bottle was right there by her bed. If it knocked her out this bad, I'd assume she took at least seven to ten pills. Chased it down with half a beer. Nine-one-one got the call an hour ago. *From* Rose. She knew what she had done and apparently had some grief about it. Changed her mind. It's the fact that she was coherent enough to make the call that makes me think her chances of pulling through are good. I *will* tell you, though, that when the medics arrived on the scene, she was unresponsive. She's *still* unresponsive but we're doing our very best to pull her through."

"Can I see her?"

"Very soon. She's only been in a room, stationary, for about five minutes. Let us finish getting her squared away and—"

"You don't understand," Avery said, feeling like her knees might fail her at any moment. "This is my fault. She did this because of me...because...."

She stuttered into a series of sobs at this point. The doctor stepped forward and braced her up with a hand to the shoulder. "Just a few more minutes and you can see her. You have my word on that."

Avery nodded and took two steps to the left. There, she placed her back against the wall and slid down to the floor. She then bent her legs, pulling her knees toward her head, and wept as quietly as she could.

***

The doctor was true to his word. Avery was allowed into the room seven minutes later. Another one of those stuttering sobs came crawling out of her throat when she stepped through the doorway. Rose was lying motionless in bed, hooked up to a breathing tube. The doctor had warned her before entering that she was unconscious and could likely remain that way for at least a day or so.

There were still two nurses in the room, one of whom gave her a heartbreaking look. The other nurse was checking Rose's vitals on a monitor that stood by the bed like a sentinel watching over the terrible scene.

Avery approached Rose's bedside and took her hand. She squeezed it lightly and slowly sank into a chair. She was dimly aware of the nurses taking their leave as she broke into a crying fit. For a moment, she felt like the fabric of space and time had torn open and spit her right back to Ramirez's bedside—when he had been coming around and sure to come home any day. Of course, that's not how it had played out. He had been murdered in his hospital bed when she was elsewhere trying to find a killer.

Of course, the hand she now held was not Ramirez's. Still, the implication was the same. Rose had done this to herself for some reason—likely for reasons closely related to her mother. The only glimmering hope in all of it was that, according to the doctor, Rose had changed her mind at the last moment and had called for help. So maybe all wasn't lost. If Rose could change her mind in such a dark moment, maybe it meant there was also hope for repair between the two of them in the future.

How about you stop worrying how you can benefit from this and worry about her getting better, you selfish bitch, she told herself.

Because when it came down to the bare bones of it all, this was her fault. She was sure a therapist or any good friend would shoo this away, claiming that their stressed relationship might have been only a small part of Rose's troubles. But Avery could still easily replay the brief visit to Rose's apartment when Rose had screamed at her to get out.

No...this was pretty much one hundred percent her fault and she just had to learn to deal with that. Maybe it had been a mistake to go back to work so soon—or at all, for that matter. She had put Rose second *again* and look what had happened.

"I didn't know what else to do..." Avery said. "Rose, I'm sorry. I didn't know where to go or what to do and without Ramirez...work seemed the only option."

She had no idea if Rose could hear her or not but admitting it all out loud was freeing. It also brought on another bought of weeping. Avery stayed there, at Rose's bedside, her daughter's limp hand held tightly in her own.

CHAPTER TWENTY TWO

Janice Saunders could feel the migraine coiling around the inner workings of her head, tightening its grip like a python. She felt it behind her right eye first, as usual. But it was stretching out to the back and then around the base of her skull. She'd had enough of them to know what was coming and was glad that her work day was over. She was walking up the steps to her porch when she felt the first real pangs of the migraine hit and her thoughts instantly turned to the ibuprofen in her medicine cabinet and the peppermint essential oil on her bedside table.

The headaches were a result of her job. As if the stress of putting together those stupid pointless government proposals wasn't bad enough, staring at a computer screen for eight to ten hours straight was certainly a culprit as well. It was so bad that Janice would sometimes even skip watching TV on the nights when she'd had a particularly bad day. She was already five episodes behind on *This Is Us* and hadn't even gotten to start the second season of *Stranger Things.*

She'd quit the damned job if it didn't pay so well. With her next paycheck floating in her mind's eye like some wavering finish line, Janice unlocked her front door. She pushed the door open, wondering if today would be the day the place no longer felt too big. Her husband had left a little over a year ago and the place still felt too big for her, like it was no longer hers. Some nights, it felt like it was trying to swallow her and—

As she pushed the door closed behind her, Janice noticed the mess that the living room was in. It made no sense at first but then a stark feeling of absolute terror seized every nerve and fiber within her body.

A series of clown faces were staring at her. Dolls, stuffed animals, cardboard cutouts that had been taped to the walls. They all smiled at her, their greasy painted grins like bloody gashes. She looked from wall to wall, like a deer caught in headlights. Her mind was too slow to reach the obvious question of where the hell they had all come from. In that moment, terror was all she knew.

There were at least thirty clown faces looking at her. They had been propped on her sofa, sitting on the bar area that separated the living room from the kitchen, on the living room floor. Some were

101

the so-called cute antique clowns with jolly smiles. Others were the more menacing kind that newer generations had claimed as their own thanks to Stephen King.

She felt a scream rising up in her throat. She hoped that when it came out, it would unfreeze her knees so she could get the hell out of there. But with the scream came logic.

Someone put these here, she thought. *Someone broke into your house and put them here. And they know about your thing with clowns...This is a mean prank, a very mean prank, and whoever broke into your house might still be here and—*

That's when a figure rose up from behind the bar from the kitchen side. They'd been hiding there the whole time. It was the figure of a man, dressed in a black hoodie and sweatpants. She did not see his face because it was covered by a clown mask. The skin of it was a mottled gray and the sinister smile stretched from one side to the other, impossibly wide.

The man behind the mask let out a high-pitched giggling noise. And then he brought out the knife.

Still giggling manically, the clown climbed over the bar with insane agility, the knife raised in the air. Tufts of colorful hair flowed out behind him like pure nightmare fuel. Seeing this, that's when Janice's bladder let go.

Perhaps it was the warm trickle running down her legs that finally broke her free. With her heart slamming like a caged animal in her chest, Janice turned and headed for the door. Her hand was about three inches away from the knob when the knife plunged into her back, just below her right shoulder blade.

The pain was sharp and immense, particularly when the blade clanged against the bone of her shoulder. She cried out, partially in pain and partially the bloodcurdling scream her lungs had been working on for the last several seconds. She felt the knife pull away but then it was in her again, this time lower. Then again and again.

Her legs gave out and she went hard to the floor. The clown was on her, rolling her over onto her back. As it straddled her, her first fear was that she was going to be raped, but that was a fleeting worry. In a pool of her own urine and quickly spilling blood, she realized that the clown had other things on his mind.

The clown giggled again, his large face maddeningly close to her own as his little legion of dolls watched from behind him. He raised the knife and brought it down. She counted four times before a dim sort of darkness finally crept in front of her eyes. The last shuddering thought in Janice's mind was if she had actually stayed alive long enough to actually feel her heart stop.

102

CHAPTER TWENTY THREE

Avery knew how hospital time was somehow intangible; it seemed to flow differently when you were at the bedside of a loved one. It was more than just time that seemed off, though. Her body did, too. She knew she should sleep but she was not tired. She knew that she should eat but she was not hungry.

She checked her phone. Six missed calls, three texts. All from Kellaway, O'Malley, and Connelly. She didn't bother checking them just yet. She was more interested in the time. She wasn't all that surprised to find that it was one in the morning.

Rose's condition had not changed. She was still unconscious, still relying on the breathing tube. But her doctor said her vitals were strong and he was now confident to say she'd be out of the woods sooner rather than later. As she looked at Rose, Avery thought about the conversation she'd had with the doctor during his last rounds before he had left for the day.

He had brought Avery a sandwich from the cafeteria which she had barely nibbled at. He'd pulled up the chair from the corner of the room and took a seat.

"I'm going to level with you and I hope you'll understand the blatant nature of it. You being a detective, I assume you deal in hard facts, right?"

"Right."

"Well, based on what I know about these kinds of situations, I think this was really just a cry for help. Even if she didn't know it...I think that's what it is. If she really wanted to do some damage, she would have taken more pills. The EMTs on the scene said there were about a dozen or so left in the bottle. And she also wouldn't have called for help. I only tell you this to let you know that she may need you to dig the issues out of her when she's back to normal—or as close to normal as you can get after something like this."

Avery thought: *Rose won't want me digging for anything.* But she said nothing of the sort. She simply nodded and considered the doctor's advice.

That had been about seven hours ago. And while she was still thinking over what he had said, she didn't think there was that much hope when it came to her and Rose. Avery had never been

103

particularly close to her mother; after the age of twenty-one or so, they'd simply grown apart. Maybe that was the future she had with Rose. Maybe she just needed to accept it.

To keep her mind busy and away from the horrors of her personal future, she read through the texts and emails that had come in. Every text had asked if they could help in any way. Kellaway included a side note to let Avery know that she'd be praying for her and Rose and that if she needed a shoulder for the late-night hours, to text her.

It was not much, but to see such support from people who, for the most part, had remained constants in her life—as well as a new face—made her think that maybe her world had not been wiped out when Ramirez had died. Why had she felt such a need to wipe her slate clean and start over from the beginning? Why had she gone into hiding anyway?

Because you were retreating, she told herself. *You were only thinking about yourself. Rose's father dies and you move farther away. What kind of messed up shit is that?*

Avery's final thought before she finally drifted off to sleep in the uncomfortable chair was that maybe she'd had it backward all along. She'd assumed Rose would need a lot of help to pull through her father's death and the trauma of the case that had taken his life. When, in reality, Avery was starting to realize she might be the one who needed the most help of all.

***

The buzzing of her phone woke her up at 7:10 that morning. There was an ache in her neck from having fallen asleep in the chair and a nasty taste in her mouth from not having had a chance to brush her teeth. The number on her phone's display screen was one she recognized but had not programmed in yet. It was Kellaway.

She answered it, her heart warmed by Kellaway's kind offers via text. There was no sense in shutting her out. It would solve nothing and only make her seem unapproachable.

"Hey, Kellaway," she said.

"Hi," Kellaway said. "How's she doing?"

"She's still out of it but the doctors think she'll pull through."

"I thought you should know that O'Malley and Finley got worried about you. They pulled the reports from the EMTs. So they know what happened. I do, too. But no one else. I feel like we were snooping and I'm sorry."

"It's okay. Really. Look…are you okay to stay on the case while I'm here?"

"Yeah. I'm meeting with Connelly to talk about it later this morning. But hopefully you'll be back on it soon."

"We'll see," Avery said.

"Anyway, I thought you might want an update. We were able to find Abby Costello's old phone. It was in one of the ecoATMs a few blocks away from her apartment. It was worse than just the cracked screen we were told about. It was pretty badly broken. The tech guys say it looks like she wiped it out. They can pull up the call logs, but it might take a while."

"So maybe she just never got a chance to program the new one before her date," Avery said thoughtfully.

"Most likely. Also, the first guy Abby saw at the restaurant checks out. Turns out, though, it was his first date with her. Met her on Tinder. They got into an argument when she told him point-blank he wasn't her type and had no intentions of seeing him again after having a few drinks. He cut out and went to see a movie with a friend. He showed me the ticket stub and the text messages thread with the friend. So he's clean."

"Good work."

Kellaway paused for a moment, as if she wanted to say something else, but eventually just decided on: "Please let me know if you need anything."

"I will. Thanks."

They ended the call like that and Avery could not help but hate herself a bit for wishing that she could be out there on the hunt. But she looked at Rose, in bed with the breathing tube still attached, and knew that if she was going to get her life in order, she was going to have to work on her priorities.

***

A little less than two hours later, Rose opened her eyes. She made a series of gasping noises, as she was unfamiliar with the breathing tube and alarmed at finding herself in a strange room. With the assistance of two nurses and her doctor, she was tube-free and resting as easily as she could half an hour later.

While a nurse spoke with her and checked her vitals, Avery and the doctor hung by the doorway outside. It was killing Avery to not be in there with her daughter, but she did her best to remain patient and calm.

105

"She's responding splendidly to all stimuli," the doctor said. "She'll be groggy for quite some time and although she will likely be very hungry, we'll have to feed her slowly. We'd like to keep her overnight, but I don't see any reason to worry. Like I said...just be there for her in the coming days as she starts to explore the reasons behind what she did. I'd be happy to recommend a psychiatrist if you think it might help."

Avery thanked him and watched as he made his way down the hallway. She turned back toward the room, peeking in. The nurse motioned her inside and when they passed one another—Avery on the way into the room and the nurse on the way out—the nurse gave her a hopeful little smile.

"Hey there, kiddo," Avery said.

"Hey, Mom..."

And that was all it took. Rose's bottom lip trembled and she started crying. They were deep, hitching sobs that seemed to come from her heart. She reached out with a trembling arm for Avery and Avery was more than happy to oblige. She went to Rose's side and took her in her arms with caution.

"It's okay, sweetie," Avery said. "It's okay. I'm so sorry. I should have been there for you. You should have been able to know that I would be there no matter what and—"

"No," Rose said. "I'm so sorry. This is on me, Mom. I was being stupid and selfish and I wanted to hate you so bad. I needed to blame you and..."

The words were lost in her tears, becoming nothing more than slurred sounds. Avery started to weep softly then and for the better part of ten minutes, that's how their reunion went: two women, having shared grief with one another and seeking a new way to continue with their lives, finding the answer had been right in front of them the entire time.

***

Nurses came in and out of the room like bees revolving around a hive. From what they shared with Avery, things were looking very positive. Their cheerful demeanor seemed to rub off on Rose; within an hour of their crying session, Rose seemed to have it together. She would smile politely at the nurses and was able to lock eyes with her mother without breaking out into tears.

Just before noon, Avery sat on the edge of the bed and took Rose's hand. She'd decided to just go for it—to be as up front and as honest as possible.

106

"So, the doctor says this was a cry for help," she said. "What do you think of that?"

"I hope it wasn't," she said. "I...I don't know. I'd thought about it a few times since Dad died. But it was always just this escapist fantasy bullshit. God...you know me, Mom. Suicide is such a stupid thing. Poor little girl, can't handle the stress. And to make it worse, I chose pills. Lame. It could have been something harder, you know? Razorblades in the bathtub, a gun in the mouth..."

"Stop it," Avery said, each thought pasting itself onto the front of her mind.

"Sorry. But you know what I mean. Mom...my God, I'm so sorry. I don't know what I was thinking."

"I think I might," Avery said. "You were thinking that your father died because a killer your mother was chasing got to him. You were thinking that your mother is always choosing the career that consequently killed your father over you. And the hell of it is you wouldn't be wrong."

"No, that's not it. Not really. There have been days in the last few months where I missed you just as much as I missed Dad. And it's harder because you're still here, you know? I just...I don't know what it is Mom. I wish I did..."

Behind them, Avery's phone could be heard buzzing. She had silenced the ringer early last night and had not turned it on again. It was giving a series of buzzing noises, indicating that a call was coming in. Avery ignored it completely, while Rose looked over at the chair.

"It's okay, Mom. I know you might not think so, but I love the fact that you're so committed to your job. It's important. I know that and I respect that. You're a badass. I just get jealous, I think. I knew you went back to work; I saw a snippet on the news where you were rushing into the precinct. Had a new partner, from the looks of it. Not nearly as cute as Ramirez."

"That's the truth. I'm sorry, Rose. I should have called. I should have asked. But...my work is the only thing I know how to do well. I had to go back to see if it could help me get back to where I was before he died."

"I get that, Mom. And it's okay. It really is. I get it."

"Still...I don't want you to ever think I'm choosing you second."

"Mom...I'm not blind. I've seen the way you've tried to mend things between us. Several times, you've tried and I've shot you down. I was still being that naïve little girl that wanted to piss you

107

off because things with you and Dad didn't work out. I've never felt *second* because of your work, despite some of the things I might have said in the past."

"You're an amazing kid," Avery said.

"And you're a shitty detective," Rose said, nodding toward the chair where Avery's phone sat. "Answer the call. According to the news, you're apparently working on some nasty case."

"You're more important, Rose."

"Yes, we've established that," Rose said, kissing Avery's cheek. "Now go find the killer. Stop him from killing someone else."

They shared a look between them. Nothing was said, but a ton was communicated. *Go stop the killer…don't give up. Dad's dead but you caught the bastard that did it. Don't stop now. Do your job. Save lives.*

Avery gently ruffled Rose's hair and kissed her on the forehead. "We're going to be okay, Rose," she said.

"Yeah, we are," Rose said. "And I promise to do my part from here on out."

"Same here," Avery said.

She got off of the bed, feeling something strange as she picked up the phone. That feeling, she realized, was knowing that she had Rose's full support—that Rose was, in essence, her cheerleader. It was a strange feeling…a great feeling.

She saw that the call had come from O'Malley. She tried calling him back but it went to voicemail. She then pulled up Kellaway's number and tried her. As dutiful and eager to please as ever, Kellaway answered on the second ring.

"I saw that O'Malley called me five minutes ago," Avery said. "Do you know what's going on?"

"Yeah," Kellaway said. "I'm driving to the scene now. Another murder. And this one might be even weirder than the spiders."

"Where is it?" Avery asked.

She looked back at Rose for further assurance and got it in the form of a proud smile.

"Detective Black…no. Stay with your daughter. I don't want you to—"

"Give me the address," Avery said. "I'm on my way."

CHAPTER TWENTY FOUR

As it happened, the hospital was closer to the crime scene than the A1, so Avery arrived only a few moments after Kellaway. Finley was also with her, both of them with their shoulders hunched up against a drizzle of cold rain that had just started to fall. Avery got out of her car, pulled a light coat on over her own shoulders, and joined them at their cars.

The house was located on a small strip of side road that branched off from the central highway. The houses were not close together, with at least an acre or so of land separating each property. It was the sort of place that could still be referred to as a neighborhood rather than a subdivision. They started toward the house as a trio, heading toward the partially opened front door and the single police officer waiting in the doorway.

"What do we know for sure?" Avery asked.

"If it's all the same to you," Kellaway said, "I'd rather see it for myself before I try describing what I've been told."

"She's right," Finley said. "The poor guy that called it in…from what I understand, he sounded like a lunatic."

"Yeah, a coworker discovered the body about forty minutes ago," Kellaway said. "She didn't show up for work, her supervisor got pissed because they were against deadline, and he actually sent someone to her home to look for her when she wouldn't answer emails or her phone."

They had reached the porch by this point. They ducked under the yellow crime scene tape that had been strung up between the porch rails. The officer in the doorway nodded as he heard Kellaway relaying the information.

"That's right. Poor bastard had to be escorted home. He was a mess."

"And you were the first officer on the scene?" Avery asked. He was a familiar face—one she'd seen countless times but never really got to know. A slightly overweight man by the name of Hancock.

"I was," Hancock said. "And yeah…it creeped me the hell out, too. See for yourself."

Hancock stepped aside, looking to be very glad that he could step out into the fresh air.

When Avery stepped into the house, she saw that Kellaway had not been exaggerating. It looked like something straight out of a horror movie. First, the body lying in the floor was coated in blood. A pool of it expanded about two feet around in her all directions. There were stab wounds everywhere, even in the left side of the woman's jaw. A quick initial glance allowed Avery to count at least seven stab wounds.

But beyond the body, there were the clowns. So many clowns. Dolls, porcelain figurines, cardboard cutouts, stuffed figures…there were at least thirty of them and they were all looking in the direction of the front door.

"What the hell happened here?" Finley whispered.

Avery hunkered down as close as she could to the body without placing a foot into the blood. She saw that her count of seven wounds had been off. She now saw ten clearly. She wondered how many more there might be on her back. She also saw a stain that seemed inconsistent with the bloodstains, located at her crotch.

"She urinated on herself," Avery said, pointing out the dark splotch.

"And my God, look at her eyes," Kellaway said.

Avery had noticed the eyes, too. Wide open, frozen in terror. Just like Alfred Lawnbrook. Just like Abby Costello.

"We have a name?" Avery asked.

Hancock poked his head back into the house, his voice light and almost dreamlike. "Janice Saunders. In the middle of a divorce, working as a proposal specialist for some government agency in town from what I understand."

"Has anyone talked to the neighbors yet?"

Before Hancock could answer her, she heard the sound of approaching sirens as more officers arrived. She looked out of the still-opened door and saw two police cars approaching from the north, from the direction of the highway. But she also saw another vehicle not too far behind. A news van.

"Damn it," Avery said.

"How do they find out so damned fast?" Finley asked.

"There were too many people involved in this one," Avery said. "A supervisor at work and then probably a handful of employees who knew the supervisor had sent someone out to search. Add to that the fact that the news has already been on my ass for returning back and it's a perfect storm. I bet someone was tailing me the moment I left the fucking hospital."

"Vultures," Finley said.

110

"Hancock," Avery said. "Can you and Finley manage things here for a moment? Stay out until the other officers arrive. Kellaway and I are going to run over to the neighbor's and see if we can get any sort of information. I'd love to get inside before the news van sees us."

"I'm good with that," Finley said.

"Same here," Hancock said.

Avery and Kellaway made their exit right away. The police cruisers were slowing down to turn into the driveway. The shape of the news van behind them was much clearer now. Avery figured that if someone inside was really paying attention, they'd see her and Kellaway charging across the lawn to the neighbor's house.

"You ever seen anything like that?" Kellaway asked as they approached the neighbor's front porch.

"No," Avery said. "And believe me, I've seen a lot of surreal things."

Spiders...and now clowns. Avery didn't think there was any doubt now. Fear was certainly an aspect of these murders.

When they climbed the porch stairs to the neighbor's house, there was a woman already standing at the front door. She was an older woman, perhaps sixty, staring out through a glass screen door at the commotion in Janice Saunders's driveway. She took a cautious step backward as Avery and Kellaway approached. Avery showed the woman her badge and right away, the lady stepped forward and opened the door for them.

"I'm Detective Black, and this is my partner, Officer Kellaway," Avery said. "I was wondering if we might have a moment of your time—preferably before the people in those news vans notice we're over here."

"What's happened?" the woman asked.

"I can tell you the basics, but I'd really prefer that we do it inside," Avery said.

The old woman nodded and allowed them into her home. Before she closed the door behind them, she took one more look outside. From what Avery could tell, she was the reclusive elderly type that thrived on gossip. Probably the type who *wanted* the news vans and the commotion.

When the door was closed, the woman turned and frowned as if she already knew what had happened. "Has something happened to Janice?"

"I'm afraid so," Avery said. "She's been murdered."

"Oh my God..."

"Ma'am, can I get your name?"

111

"Courtney Fowler…she's been *murdered*?"

"Yes. Were you close?"

"We used to be. But her husband left her about a year ago and since then, she hasn't done much socializing. I'd try to go by to invite her over for tea or coffee but she was always very distant."

"Do you know why her husband left her?" Kellaway asked.

"I don't know for sure, but I think there was an affair of some kind. Those are the rumors I hear, anyway. That her husband got involved in an affair and chose the other woman over her."

"What do you think the chances are that the ex-husband might be capable of murder?"

Courtney had led them slowly into her living room and sat down on her couch. She removed her eyeglasses and wiped a tear away. "No…he might have been a bastard for leaving her but he's not the sort to act out in violence."

"You're certain of that?" Avery asked.

"I am. Unless he snapped at some point and I was unaware of it, he was a pretty reputable young man."

"I have another question for you," Avery said. "And it might seem a little strange. But do you happen to know if Janice had any phobias?"

Courtney thought about it for a moment before nodding slowly, a thought creeping up on her. "Actually, yes. I had a Halloween party here about two years ago, for the people in the neighborhood—a grown-up Halloween party. Janice and her husband came and they dressed up as a witch and her broom, if I recall. Anyway, the night was going splendidly and then one of our neighbors from up the street came over. Another nice couple, really. But the husband had dressed up as a clown. And when Janice saw it, she went into another room. I could tell that she was uneasy. Then when the party congregated all together in that one room—my den area, just on the other side of the living room—Janice freaked out. She was visibly frightened and borderline rude. She left right away.

"Everyone thought she was playing around, you know? So the gentleman that had dressed up as a clown started goofing around with her as she tried to leave. He blocked the door and started chuckling at her, trying to be funny. Janice screamed at him and started crying before she finally pushed him out of her way and left."

"So you'd place a safe bet on the idea that Janice was afraid of clowns?" Avery asked.

112

"Oh yes. She called me the following day to apologize. She said she knew it was a stupid and irrational fear, but she'd been scared of them for most of her life."

"Did she say why?" Kellaway asked.

"I don't believe so. But I just assumed it was something from her childhood."

Avery and Kellaway shared a look. They had gotten the information they needed and had also subsequently informed a neighbor that someone she had once known relatively well had been killed. It had only taken about five minutes but it felt much longer…it usually did when Avery had to inform someone of an untimely death.

"Can I ask how she was murdered?" Courtney asked.

"Sorry," Avery said. "Not at this stage."

But even as she and Kellaway prepared to make their exit, Avery was now more certain than ever that this killer was somehow motivated by the fear of his victims. There was no tried and true smoking gun but she thought she might find a pretty clear link with another visit to the coroner once the body of Janice Saunders was taken away.

CHAPTER TWENTY FIVE

Even before Janice's body had arrived at the morgue, Avery had placed a call to Cho Yin, requesting that one of the first things to be looked into were cortisol levels. Avery was pretty sure she knew what Yin would find, given that Janice's bladder had voided itself during whatever had happened to her.

Even Avery, who had never been scared of clowns in any way, could not shake the sight of all of those creepy little leering faces, all pointed toward the front door in Janice's house. Whoever the killer was, they were going to great lengths to terrify their victims.

Knowing that it might take up to an hour to get the results she was looking for, Avery contacted the A1. She asked for the home and cell phone numbers of Abby Costello's mother. She got her information back within five minutes: Trisha Costello lived in an upscale community near Smith Mountain Lake, Virginia. She owned a small yet successful boutique shop, which she had been running for the better part of ten years. Also, she had been informed of her daughter's death yesterday afternoon after her husband had finally worked up the nerve to call her. Trisha had then called the A1 for information about the case, demanding that it be of the utmost importance to everyone involved.

So when Avery got her on the phone, Trisha Costello was more than happy to help. She felt as if the police were taking her seriously. While there was an underlying tone of over-importance and contempt in the woman's voice, she was still as helpful as she could be.

Avery spoke with her while sitting with Kellaway, parked in front of the morgue and waiting to go in.

"I know it has to be a difficult time for you," Avery said, "but I have a few questions. Some may seem a bit odd, but I think they might potentially help us find who did this to your daughter."

"It's okay," Trisha said. "I'm actually on the way to the airport right now to go to Boston to attend the funeral."

She spoke as if she was on the phone with a client rather than discussing the murder and burial of her only daughter.

"Well, speaking with your ex-husband, we discovered that Abby had a fear of open bodies of water. I assume you were aware of this?"

"I was. Were you told about the water-skiing mishap?"

"Yes, I was. But let me ask you...once you and your ex divorced, how often did you see Abby?"

"Three times a year. Though over the last few years, we FaceTimed a few times a month."

"And how was the relationship?" Avery asked.

"Strained, I suppose. But over the last several years, it got better."

"Did she ever come to you with problems or issues that she might not have discussed with her father?"

"Well, yeah, for the woman stuff. Periods, crushes, things like that."

"So Abby actually spoke with you about men?"

"To a degree. Never any details, though. She was very private about that sort of thing."

"Did she ever mention any men that she was uneasy about? Maybe a man she was actually scared of?"

"Not that I remember," Trisha said.

"Okay, so what about the water thing? Did she ever mention it to you?"

"Actually, yes. Sometime last year, we got into a discussion about a beach trip she went on and she told me how embarrassing it was. She asked me to go over the details of the skiing incident again. So I did and when she realized that it really wasn't as traumatic as she remembered it, she asked how someone might get over a fear."

"And what did you tell her?" Avery asked.

"I told her that there were all kinds of support groups for that sort of thing. I mentioned a psychiatrist but she shot that idea down right away."

"And do you know if she ever sought the help of a support group?"

"I'm afraid I don't. We never talked about it again. I figured it was one of those ideas mothers offer that ultimately get ignored."

"I see," Avery said. "Well, that's all for now. Would you please reach back out to me if you happen to recall any details about men she might have mentioned?"

"Absolutely," Trisha said. She did not sound like a grieving woman at all, but rather like as woman who had been delegated with a task that she simply had to do.

When Avery ended the call, she saw that Kellaway was placing a call on her phone. Avery cast her a *what-are-you-up-to* glance,

115

feeling like maybe Kellaway was preoccupied with something else rather than the tasks at hand.

"Support groups," Kellaway said. "That's a great angle, I'm going to place a call to A1 and have someone compile a list of support groups that deal with phobias."

Avery smiled her approval. "Thanks."

As she listened to Kellaway place the request, once again impressed by her get-it-done attitude, Avery received a call of her own on her phone. She checked the number and found it familiar, though not yet saved.

It was Cho Yin. She had the results Avery had asked for and was requesting a quick meeting.

***

Yin had them meet her in her tiny office, tucked away in the back of the morgue but close enough to the exam rooms where it was impossible to forget what she did for a living. She already had a few different reports waiting for Avery on her tidy desk when they came into the office.

"I assume you found something interesting if you thought we should meet face-to-face?" Avery asked.

"That's putting it mildly," Yin said. "The cortisol levels were indeed spiked. But what's even crazier than that is the apparent surge of adrenaline that hit her the moment before Janice Saunders died. From what I'm seeing—and this is, of course, all just preliminary—it looks like a massive surge of adrenaline slammed through her. There's a good chance she died of a heart attack before the knife wounds did her in."

"So you're saying her fear caused a heart attack?" Avery asked.

"Possibly. The amount of adrenaline I'm speculating on would cause the heart to go crazy—to kick into overdrive. And in some cases when this happens, the heart goes into cardiac arrest."

"So she literally died of fright?" Kellaway asked.

"That or one of the eighteen stab wounds. But I've honestly never seen a case of this kind of fear-induced irregularities in an exam. I've read about them, sure, but never actually seen it with my own eyes."

"And it can actually happen?" Avery asked. "Dying of fright?"

"Yes indeed. People can literally die of broken hearts, too; that's not just an urban legend. The physiological processes of both are the same. The heart gets overwhelmed with an emotion and locks up. The trauma has to be pretty damned severe, though."

116

"So…a woman who has a genuine fear of clowns could be scared *to death* by an unexpected appearance of roughly thirty clown dolls and figurines?"

"Yes, I think it's very likely," Yin said. "And based on what I'm seeing, I'd place my money on fear. I truly believe that Janice Saunders was quite literally scared to death."

CHAPTER TWENTY SIX

Kellaway received a text from Finley as Avery opened the morgue doors and headed back to the parking lot. Avery found herself wanting to know more about Kellaway's past. While it was a little silly to assume that Kellaway was more hardened because she had spent time on the NYPD, it was clear that she had a level head on her shoulders. And it apparently took quite a bit to get under her skin.

"Is that our support group list?" Avery asked.

"It is," Kellaway said. "And surprisingly, there are only two that deal specifically with phobias. Even more surprisingly, someone at the A1 already went ahead and checked to see if any of the victims attended any of the groups."

"And?"

"Janice Saunders attended both groups. But get this...all three of our recent victims attended the second one. And here's the best part: Alfred Lawnbrook attended as recently as two weeks ago."

"You got an address?"

"I just plugged it into my GPS," Kellaway said.

Avery felt like part of a machine as she got back behind the wheel of the car. Dimly, in the back of her head, she felt a stab of guilt for being so caught up in this case when Rose was still in the hospital. Even though Rose had basically given her a blessing and a command to get back to work and bring this guy in, Avery's maternal instinct was cringing.

Maybe, she thought as she followed the instructions Kellaway gave her, *I'll work on merging those two parts of myself when this case is over. And if I can get them to coexist, it might make me a better mother...and maybe even a better detective.*

***

The support group met several times a week. The most prominent one was after hours, on Wednesday and Thursday evenings according to the placard in the window of Room 3A of the Etheredge Community Center. As Avery's luck would have it, today's meeting was at noon just twenty minutes shy of the moment she and Kellaway parked in front of the building.

118

Kellaway had called the center to get the name of the group leader. Luck was on their side there, as well. The primary lead counselor for the weekday group was already in the meeting room, brewing the coffee and setting up chairs. She said she'd be happy to meet with Avery and Kellaway before the meeting.

When they entered Room 3A, the coffee was brewing and a very pretty middle-aged woman was setting up a tray with crackers, cheese, and chips on a table in the back. The room and the way it was set up was what Avery imagined Alcoholic Anonymous meetings might look.

The woman turned to them and gave a bright, genuine smile. They knew her name from the call—Delores Moon. She was fifty-one but looked significantly younger. She was dressed professionally, as if she might be heading back to her office when the group was over, but also not too stuffy. She looked warm and welcoming—probably a necessity for an environment like this.

"Thanks so much for meeting with us," Avery said. "I know it must be stressful to lead something like this."

"It can be at times. But the weekday crowds tend to be small. And I thought about it after speaking with you...people with phobias aren't like the majority of people that attend support groups. With most other issues that require attention or support, people are typically hesitant to share about their problems. But people that suffer from intense fear of things tend to *want* to talk about it. It makes them feel like they can maybe better understand it and, as such, get a grip on it."

"That makes sense," Kellaway said.

"I say all of that," Moon said, "because I think the people that will start coming in here in a few minutes wouldn't mind you sitting in on the meeting—especially not if you tell them why you're here. Especially Alfred's case...it's been a point of conversation with a few of the regulars. I've gotten several calls and emails. Alfred wasn't much for sympathizing with others, but he was really starting to make progress towards overcoming his fears. It seemed liked it, anyway."

"And what about Abby Costello and Janice Saunders?"

"Well, Janice has been struggling with hers for a while. She was truly embarrassed by it. At first it was just scary clowns. She was literally traumatized for about a week when one of her childhood friends made her watch *It*—you know, the Stephen King movie with the clown? But more digging revealed that she'd seen a clown on stilts fall at a carnival. When he got up his face was all bloody and he was screaming. Something about that moment

119

altered something in her mind and she was legitimately terrified of clowns. It hurts my heart to hear that she died."

Avery nodded, fully aware that Moon had not yet heard about *how* Janice Saunders had died. She almost told her then and there but the murder was so new that it would almost feel like a security breach. Of course, given why they were here, Avery assumed Moon could probably figure it out easily enough.

"So, you just said that people with phobias tend to *want* to talk about their fears," Avery said. "But based on the cases we've been seeing, a lot of family and friends say that the victims were usually hesitant."

"Yes, admitting it to those closest to you can be hard. It's embarrassing for some. But once you get around people you know can sympathize with what you have always thought of as irrational fears…it makes you feel safe. It makes you feel *normal*."

Avery thought of Alfred Lawnbrook, escaping to the butterfly garden at the museum. Had he been escaping or maybe looking for someone who knew about spiders to ask them questions in the hopes of better understanding them? It would certainly explain why he entered into the relationship with Stefon Scott.

"Do you think some of them would be open to having us ask questions about the victims?"

"I think they'd actually invite it," Moon said. "With what Alfred and Abby experienced in their deaths, these are people who feel that the victims are being targeted because of their fears. It's quite personal to them."

At that comment, a man with a scraggly beard entered the room. Moon welcomed him warmly and when she introduced them, she was very careful not to provide the man's name. Avery got it; in her profession, confidentiality was very important. Avery let it go. She didn't think she'd need names unless someone was able to provide something really concrete.

His arrival broke up the conversation. Within a few minutes, another person entered the room, an overweight woman of about sixty. Again, Moon made introductions without giving the attendee's name. She did make it clear, however, that Avery and Kellaway were here from the Boston PD Homicide Division, trying to find the person who had killed Alfred, Abby, and, most recently, Janice. No one had heard the news of Janice yet and two of the people that filed in as noon approached seemed to take the news like a punch to the gut.

By 12:02, there were seven attendees in the room. They had grabbed their cups of coffee and their plates of snacks and sat in the semicircle of metal folding chairs Moon had set up prior to their arrival. Three of the attendees did not seem all that thrilled that there were outsiders present. They'd said nothing during introductions and Avery could read in their body language— crossed arms and all but pinned to the backs of their chairs—that they would be no help. One of these three had been thoroughly devastated by the news of Janice's murder.

Delores Moon was unfazed, though. She stood in the center of the semicircle like a teacher in front of her class. And the seven attendees all looked up to her with reverence and hope.

"Today is going to be different," Moon said. "I've introduced you to our guests. And I know that we have all felt the losses of our three friends. We may not have known them all very well, but they shared a heartache that you all have in common. We've discussed this and know the importance of it. So today, I want those of you that are confident and self-assured to help our guests—Detective Black and Officer Kellaway—to understand the nature of what you go through on a daily basis. How do your fears affect your lives? What would you tell someone off the street what it's like? How would you describe your fears and their effects on your life?

"The hope is that they can use your descriptions to better understand the mindset of someone who *preys* on people with genuine fears. So please don't hold back. So many of you have been admirable in how open and vulnerable you've been. Please…help these courageous women to bring this horrid killer to justice."

There was less than two seconds of silence before someone spoke up. It was the bearded man who had been the first to arrive. When he spoke, all eyes turned in his direction. Some in attendance looked frightened at what he might say. Others looked at him with awe and a bit of jealousy.

"Hell, I don't mind," he said. "The clinical word for my fear is thanatophobia—the fear of dying. And not just the *act* of dying, of one day just not being alive anymore. It's thinking that just about anything could kill me. The cab ride over here. The cold I had two weeks ago. Falling off the treadmill at the gym. The elevator in my building breaking and crashing down five floors. I live with these fears every day. But not just like these small, passing fears. I avoid the elevator at all costs, even when I have a ton of groceries to go up to my apartment. Whenever I get sick, it feels one hundred times worse because I think everything can kill me. Even right now, I'm *very* aware of the guns on your hips and I'm wondering how they might accidentally go off by themselves. Logically, I know they can't. But I'm still basically terrified that you're in this room."

Almost right away, another attendee spoke up. This was a younger woman—probably younger than thirty. She was squirming in her seat, clearly anxious.

"Everything he said...but with fire. I'm terrified of fire. I have never once in my life enjoyed a hot bath because I think the intense heat could somehow ignite something in the bathroom. I avoid any sort of hair accessories for the same reason—hair dryers, curling irons, you name it. I shit you not...everything in my apartment is flame proof. I have one of those convection stoves where everything is heated by magnets—a convection oven—because the thought of a burner on a stove makes me puke. And I meant that literally—I've actually thrown up at my family's Thanksgiving dinner because of the burners on the stove and the candles lit on the dining room table."

Avery admired the courage it took for these people to be so open and honest with what they perceived as serious flaws. She had her own baggage and knew what it was like to try to air it out for others. Still, as she listened, she was in detective mode; she was looking for anyone who stood out more than the others. Maybe someone who looked almost unbearably uncomfortable because there were police in attendance. Perhaps an attendee who shifted in an anxious way when the murders of their former group members came up.

But Avery could spot nothing of the sort.

"Let me ask you," Avery said, addressing the room. "Is there anyone other than Janice that is usually here that is not here today?"

"None of the regulars from what I can see," Moon said.

"Yeah, if you don't count the dropouts," one of the men who had remained silent to this point said.

"Dropouts?" Kellaway asked.

"A few people try us out and find out that we go deep quickly," said the woman who was afraid of fire. "The most recent one was a guy named—"

"No names, please," Moon said, clearly a little annoyed.

"Well, he had what I thought was a made up fear—a fear of being afraid. The idea of being scared...well, it scared him. But at the same time, he thought *our* phobias were stupid."

"Yes," Moon said, "yet for the sake of confidentiality, we can't discuss such things because that person is not here."

"I understand that," Avery said, "but if this is someone who was here for a few weeks and then left without much notice— especially in the last few weeks—it could be very important to the case. At the very least, it could provide a lead."

Moon looked around at the assembled group as if she were disappointed. She then focused on Avery and Kellaway. "Can I have a private word with you out in the hall?"

Without waiting for an answer, Moon walked to the door and out of the room. Avery and Kellaway followed. Avery was very aware of slight murmuring behind them as the group snickered. She even heard someone say *"Ah hell, looks like they're in trouble..."*

Outside of the room, Moon stepped away from the doorway so as to not be overheard by the group's prying ears.

"We have people come for a few weeks and never come back," she said. "It's nothing out of the ordinary."

"But the lady that is scared of fire seems to have been quite upset about this latest guy."

"Yes, and she has reason to. He name-called and antagonized everyone. I had a talk with him after the second week and told him if he didn't stop, he would no longer be welcomed back."

"And did he come back?" Avery asked.

"He did. And when he did, he came with a lighter. He flicked the flame open directly in front of her face. There was an altercation and I asked him to leave. He did, but he was back the following week. I threatened to call the police and he left willingly enough. I haven't seen him since then."

"I understand that with what you do here, you hold confidentiality above everything else," Avery said. "But someone that behaved like that in this environment right around the time these murders started...it has to be checked out."

Moon nodded, but solemnly. She agreed but was not happy about it. "He had what is known as phobophobia—the fear of being afraid. And from the brief time I spent with him, it was clear that he believes that in order to get over his fear, he must *create* fear to desensitize himself. Creating it for others mostly, but also putting himself in fearful situations from time to time."

"Ms. Moon...clearly you see how someone like that would be a suspect," Avery pushed.

"All I have is a name and a phone number," Moon said, admitting defeat. "That's all he put on his form...and I'm pretty sure the phone number is a fake."

"It doesn't matter," Avery said. "The name is all we need."

With a sigh, Moon gave them a name and then, without another word, she turned away and headed back into the room. The look on her face as she turned away was one of sadness; she felt as if she had betrayed someone's confidence.

123

Avery was fine with betraying confidence, honestly. She was more worried about saving lives...and if a few people had to be exposed along the way, then so be it.

CHAPTER TWENTY SEVEN

The man's name was Dan Hudson. A quick call to the A1 supplied them with his address—which turned out to be just fifteen minutes away from the community center. When Avery parked the car in front of his house, which was tucked in between two other nearly identical houses in the cheaper end of a middle-class subdivision, it was clear that he was home. Loud music was coming from inside and they could see someone walking back and forth in front of the window that looked in onto the living room. The blinds were drawn but the shape moving back and forth was easily seen.

As they got out of the car and headed for the front door, Avery was rather surprised to realize that she knew the music that was being played. It was a band Rose had been into once upon a time, some German rock outfit called Rammstein. This realization made her grin and it also turned her mind back to Rose. If she had the time, she'd go back to the hospital tonight to check in on her, no matter what the end result of this visit to Dan Hudson might be.

Avery stood back a few steps while Kellaway knocked on the door. She knocked loudly so she could be heard over the music. After a few moments the music came to an end and they could hear heavy footfalls coming to the door. When the door was finally opened, it only opened partially. With about six inches of open space, a man peeked out.

"Who are you?" he asked.

Avery showed her badge, as did Kellaway, although Kellaway's standard police uniform made it a redundant gesture. "I'm Detective Black, with Boston PD Homicide," Avery said. "We're looking for Dan Hudson. Is that you?"

"It is. Was my music too loud or something?"

"Honestly, yes. But that's not why we're here. I wonder if we might come in and ask you a few questions?"

Dan eyed them suspiciously with his one eye that peered through the crack in the door. "What's it about?" he asked and with that, Avery could hear the first signs of fear in his voice.

"We want to ask you some questions about the support group you had been attending over the last few weeks," Avery said.

"Seriously?" he said, opening the door a bit wider. "Did Delores end up calling the police anyway?"

125

"She didn't, actually," Avery said. "We ended up visiting her for a different matter."

This seemed to ease Dan's mind a bit and he finally opened the door the rest of the way. It was still clear that he was very uncomfortable, though. "Come on in," he said.

When they stepped inside, Avery found the house in nearly immaculate—albeit bland—shape. There were no pictures on the walls, no lamps, no decorations. She wondered if this had to do with his fear. Perhaps the fewer items in his house, the less afraid he was.

"So what do you need to know?" Dan asked. "If you ask me, they were the biggest bunch of crybabies I'd ever seen. Scared of *everything.*"

"And why were you there?" Kellaway asked.

"Phobophobia. Scared that I might get scared. It's not like a permanent thing. It comes and goes but when it's here, it hits hard. I was looking for help with it and ironically, seeing how those people freak out about weird stuff...well, it sort of made me feel better."

He had led them into his living room. There was no TV, only one armchair and an old couch. The old-model stereo that had been blasting the music moments ago sat in the floor, the cords neatly tucked away behind the speakers.

"How many weeks did you attend the support group?" Avery asked.

"Three weeks. I was asked to leave on the fourth week."

"And when was that?"

"Two weeks ago, I suppose."

"And other than finding comfort in the fears of others, did the group help you?" Avery asked.

"Look, it wasn't like I was mocking them."

"From what I hear, you waved a lighter in the face of a woman who has a legitimate fear of fire. That seems like mocking. It actually seems rather aggressive."

"I thought I was helping. With me, exposure to fear seems to make the phobia weaken. It loosens its grip on me."

There was another whole line of questioning behind this thought, and Avery knew that it would lead down a rabbit trail. So, trying to stick to the most basic and informative line of questioning, she asked: "During your time with the group, did you get to know Alfred Lawnbrook, Abby Costello, or Janice Saunders?"

Dan nodded his head as he plopped down in the armchair. "Yeah. I met all of them. Alfred was actually pretty cool. I mean…who the hell *isn't* scared of spiders? But Abby…her thing was water, right? I mean…what the hell? How do you take a bath?"

"Would you say you identified with Alfred because the idea of spiders scared you? And if they scare you, then that represents *your* phobia, right?"

"No, I didn't identify with him. There *was* one week where he and I went out and had a beer after the group. But we weren't friends or anything like that."

"And what were your thoughts on Janice Saunders?"

"I didn't really know her that well. I don't even know if she ever revealed to the group what it was she was afraid of. Not while I was there anyway."

"And what about you?" Avery asked. "Do you recall a moment in your life when you first became aware of your fears?"

He shook his head and, unless she was imagining it, Avery was pretty sure there was a flicker of fear that came over his face. When he looked to her, she still saw it. For some reason, directing the conversation back to his own fears was setting him off.

"I don't know. Started when I was a kid I guess. But no…there was never any one moment."

"You seemed a little frightened for a while when you answered the door," Kellaway said. "Was that because you thought Delores Moon might have decided to call the cops on you after all?"

"No," he said. "I'm always like that." He seemed even more anxious now, squirming slightly in his chair. It was almost like watching him morph into something else—like watching a man start the transition into becoming a werewolf.

"Like what?" Avery asked.

"A knock on the door. A telephone call. You never know who it is, you know? You never know why they might be there. This world sucks, you know? People can be mean for no reason."

"So the uncertainty of a knock on the door scares you?"

Dan frowned and nodded. He seemed to be trying to push himself back into the armchair, visibly uncomfortable now.

"I…I need to ask you to leave now," he said. "It's coming again and it's not good. It's never good…"

"What's coming?" Avery asked.

"I shouldn't have let you in. I knew it was a bad idea and…"

"Dan, it's okay," Avery said, lowering her voice and trying to stay as consistent and non-threatening as she could. "We just need to know if—"

"Are you afraid of anything, Detective?" he asked, leering at Avery. She saw where he was beginning to sweat and for the first time, Avery started to grow nervous. She was nowhere near a psychiatrist and she was afraid she might have pushed Dan a little too far without knowing it.

"I am," she said.

"What is it?"

Losing my daughter, she thought but kept it to herself.

He smiled nervously at her. "See...not so fun to talk about what scares you, is it? I don't know what you want, but please...leave."

"Mr. Hudson," Avery said. "We can not only help you with what you're going through with your fear, but you might even be able to help us find a killer."

"A killer?" he said, stark terror now entering his voice. He said it as if the killer might very well be hiding somewhere in his house. Avery saw something like lunacy in his eyes and was pretty sure she had inadvertently pushed him over some sort of line.

That's when she saw why he had been squirming so much. He hadn't only been pushing himself into the chair as a way to symbolically retreat from the conversation; his hand had been reaching for something.

With a catlike reflex, Dan came up with a handgun. All Avery saw was a flash of black, moving upward. Dan screamed as he brought it up.

Then Avery saw another flash. It was Kellaway, launching herself forward. She collided with Dan and the chair at just about the same moment Dan pulled the trigger. Avery's hand went for her Glock but it was impulse only. As she hit the ground for cover, she was fairly certain she heard the whir of Dan's shot go sailing by her head, missing her by no less than two inches.

From the floor, Avery watched as the armchair, Kellaway, and Dan Hudson all went rocking back to the floor. Dan cried out in absolute horror, his feet kicking in the air while Kellaway expertly wrapped herself around him, applying a rear-naked choke.

Avery got to her feet and went to assist. She felt adrenaline thrumming through her body, her nerves electric. *I almost just died,* she thought. *And I should have seen him going for that gun. I missed it...and he almost killed me as a result.*

Together, Avery and Kellaway cuffed Dan and got him to his feet. He was crying a series of apologies as they led him out of his house.

"Thank you," Avery whispered to Kellaway after they had secured Dan in the back of the car.

"Of course," Kellaway said. "No problem."

"No…really. Kellaway, you saved my life back there."

For some reason, saying this out loud brought a sting of tears to her eyes. It also brought back the memory of coming one second away from blowing her own brains out before being interrupted by Howard Randall's package.

"Well, just keep in mind for the future," Kellaway said, doing her best to play down the heroics. "I'm sure if we work together after this, you'll have the chance to repay the favor."

Avery gave a lazy nod of her head, still trying to figure out why she was so struck by the realization that her life could have easily ended two minutes ago. It hadn't been the first close call in her career—not by a long shot.

She thought of Ramirez's grave, of seeing Jack's body on his living room floor, and of Rose, lying in a hospital bed half an hour away.

These things were all testaments to the fact that death was much more tangible than she had thought. Life had dealt her a harsh hand over the last few months—so harsh that perhaps she had been blinded by how precious life truly was.

She got behind the wheel and sped toward A1, anxious to get Dan Hudson in an interrogation room. And while that was prominent on her mind, it was not the most important thing.

She wanted him tucked away in a room so she could go visit her daughter a quickly as she could. Just thinking about her made tears spill down her face. She wiped them away quickly, before Kellaway could see them, while the man who had nearly killed her still wept in the back seat.

129

CHAPTER TWENTY EIGHT

Avery quickly came to realize that Dan Hudson was indeed guilty of something, in addition to having just fired at an officer: he was guilty of being an asshole.

He was still clearly terrified when he sat in the interrogation room. Avery had just come out from questioning him and had gotten little more than the same things he had offered up at his house. Connelly, Kellaway, and O'Malley watched him in the monitor. He was mewling like a scaredy cat and shifting uncomfortably in the seat.

"The guy seems like a certifiable nut job," Connelly said.

"That not exactly the PC way to put it," Avery said. "But you're not too far off. The counselor at the support group described his condition as phobophobia. He's literally scared of being scared."

"Well, that seems to be plenty of motive for going after people because of their fears," Connelly said. "It's also damning that he's willingly admitting to knowing all of the victims in some capacity."

Avery nodded. It *was* damning. And on paper, Dan Hudson would surely seem like a likely suspect. The fact that he had fired a gun at her less than an hour ago made it an even more appealing case. The more she watched him squirm in the monitor, the more she wondered if he *was* the killer. But there were a few things that stalled that notion.

For starters, while Delores Moon was not the most pleasant lady, she knew her stuff. Based on Moon's background and the trust the people in the group had in her, Avery felt safe in knowing that if she had suspected Dan Hudson as the killer, she would have said so from the start.

"I want another crack at him before anyone books him for the murders," Avery said.

Connelly smiled. "Good to see the perfectionist in you didn't go wandering away during your time off," he said.

Avery slowly walked back into the interrogation room, coming up with a line of questions that would either nail Dan to the wall or clearly show that he was innocent. She also knew, though, that she tended to do better with interrogations on the fly. As she walked into the room, she could almost feel the eyes on her in the monitor within the viewing room. She walked into the interrogation room, quickly looked up to the camera in the corner, and then took the seat across from the small table Dan Hudson currently sat behind.

"Listen, Mr. Hudson," she said. "I know you're scared and don't want to be here. And the sooner we can clear you of these murders, the sooner we can release you. You understand that, right?"

Dan's face went through a wide range of emotions, as if he couldn't decide which emotion to settle on. He finally decided on what looked like fearful content. "Don't you get it?" he said in a shaky voice. "How the hell would I murder someone? I have a legitimate and diagnosed phobia that keeps me scared of just about anything. The thought of even handling a knife scares me. All the knives in my home are butter knives because anything with sharp points has the potential to scare me. Even meeting new people is scary for me because I never know their intentions."

"Is that why you insist on insulting the people in Delores Moon's support group?" Avery asked. "Is that why you taunted one member with a lighter?"

"I don't know," he said. "I just....seeing other people scared makes me think my problem isn't so bad. Sometimes I go online and watch reaction videos on YouTube...when people react to horror movies in real time. I'll watch those scare pranks, too. Seeing people scared makes me feel...normal, I guess."

"So am I supposed to just believe that you keep your bullying of people to immature acts like flicking a lighter in a woman's face? How do I know you don't set up elaborate pranks yourself just so you can watch people get scared? You just admitted that seeing other terrified makes you feel better."

"You're not listening!" Dan said. "Everything—*every fucking thing*—has the potential to scare me. The handcuffs you put me in, this bland room, the evil way everyone has looked at me since you got me here. My mind plays out these scenarios...about how you'll beat the shit out of me to get some sort of confession or how I'll end up in jail and get raped daily. Just t-t-talking about it makes m-me...makes me go there."

Avery was pretty sure he was being genuine. No matter how good of an actor Dan might be, there was no way he was good enough to convey the sheer terror that was slowly creeping into his features.

"Here's what we're going to do," Avery said. "I'm going to take you at your word. And in a few moments, someone else will come in and work with you to come up with alibis—to see where you were and what you were doing around the time these murders

131

were committed. If all of that checks out, you won't be charged with any murders. However…I have to be honest with you: you fired at a cop and that's bad news. I'm telling you this not to scare you, but to let you start to process it. Do you understand what I'm saying?"

Dan's bottom lip started quivering and for a moment, he looked like a scared little kid sitting on the edge of his bed, waiting for his parents to check the closet for monsters. He nodded and started to let out more of this whining noises. He started to tremble and there was a noticeable hitching to his breath.

"Dan? Are you okay? Do you need help?"

"Water," he managed to say through what Avery felt was certain to be a vicious bout of sobbing on the way.

She got up quickly and left the room, hurrying back into the viewing room where O'Malley, Connelly, and Kellaway were still watching.

"He faking it?" O'Malley asked.

"No. He's in bad shape." She looked directly to Connelly and said, "I don't think he did it. I know the motive is there and it looks neat and wrapped up, but he doesn't have it in him to kill anyone."

"You sure?"

"Pretty sure, yeah. Can you get someone to line up his alibis, just to make sure? And maybe get Delores Moon on the phone. He's terrified, Connelly. He's going to need someone to talk this through when it's all said and done."

"He shot at you," Connelly said. "This won't be over for him for a long time."

Kellaway headed for the door, sensing the urgency of the situation on the screen. "I'll take him his water. I'll call Moon, too."

Avery nodded her thanks. She felt responsible for pushing him too hard, for making him resort to the reaction that she could still see on the monitor in front of her.

"If he's not the killer," Connelly said, "are there any more leads?"

She almost said *no*, but she felt like there might be something else to look into. She wasn't sure that she had missed anything per se, but maybe there were certain avenues that had not been explored yet. She thought back to the support group, all of those hopeful and needy eyes looking toward Delores Moon.

And then, strangely enough, she thought of Howard Randall's letter.

Who are you, Avery?

"Avery?" O'Malley said. "What is it?"

132

Apparently, she'd been deep in thought and it had been plastered all over her face. "Nothing," she said. "I'll be I touch and readily available, but I need to go back to the hospital. I need to check on Rose."

Connelly sighed and looked back to the monitor, then to Avery once again. "Avery...thanks for coming on for this. You've already helped immensely. But maybe you should step away. Be with your daughter and get things right there..."

"No. Just...keep me posted on *anything*."

"Are you sure?"

But she didn't bother with a response. She was already to the doorway with her thoughts on Rose in a hospital bed and that itching sort of feeling that came over her when she thought of Howard's letter. She then saw the woman from the group that was afraid of fire and the man that was afraid of death. What other phobias had been in that room? And how were they all connected other than through fear?

There's something there...something to that, she thought.

She pried at the thought as she headed to her car, feeling that maybe she *had* missed something after all. But with the need to see Rose so strong on her heart, she wasn't able to figure it out.

Avery was well aware that she had relied on Howard as something of a crutch in the past, visiting him whenever a case got too far away from her. He'd sometimes provide insight and other times make her feel foolish. But now that he was gone (apparently living somewhere else while keeping a close eye on her), she felt almost empty.

Who are you, Avery?

She'd thought she'd always known the answer to that. But leave it to Howard Randall to make her doubt it.

And in his absence, Avery thought the answer might be in a hospital bed within the heart and mind of her daughter.

CHAPTER TWENTY NINE

She arrived at the hospital just after eight o'clock. She found Rose in much better spirits, watching television and snacking on cafeteria Jell-O. The smile she gave Avery when she walked in was bright and unexpected.

"Hey," Rose said. "Back so soon? Did you close that case?"

Avery sat down in the visitor's chair and shook her head. "No, not yet. I'm trying to sort things out right now."

"Here?" Rose asked. "I'd think it would be easier to think and sort things out in a warm tub of water with a tall glass of wine."

"That does sound nice," Avery said. "How about you? How are you doing?"

"Good. The doctor checked in on me for the last time a few hours ago before clocking out for the day. He said everything looks good. They're going to release me in the morning so long as all of my bloodwork comes back normal. They want to make sure all of the meds have been flushed out of my system."

Avery cringed at how light-hearted Rose seemed when talking about it. She knew this was an opening to have a lengthier conversation but she wasn't sure how to start it. It was just as tricky as the interrogation she had just left.

"Rose...I understand the animosity you must have felt. But I want to know what I can do to make sure that you can come to me if you ever feel that way again. I'll be honest with you...I blamed myself. And maybe that was for the best. Maybe it was true."

"No, it wasn't all on you. But...not to make light of it, that really long sleep I was in was cathartic. I woke up and saw you here and something struck me."

"What's that?"

Rose was tearing up. She looked away from her mother and to the television where some terrible reality show was on. "I'm tired of being angry at you. The whole teenage angst thing should have stopped years ago. I need to stop blaming you for everything and start looking at the world through a hate-free lens. Sounds deep, sure, but that's how I feel."

"That sounds good," Avery said.

"So...I know I'm not Ramirez but do you want to tell me about this case? Why haven't you cracked it yet?"

"Cracked it?"

Rose shrugged. "I only know the lingo from what I see on TV. And let's be honest, it's all very badly written."

"I brought a suspect in this afternoon but I'm ninety percent sure he's not the guy."

"The spider guy?"

Avery chuckled, a noise that turned into a yawn. She had gone three months without these high-stress days. Today had taken its toll on her. In fact, it was all running together for her. Kneeling by Abby Costello's body by Jamaica Pond and walking into Janice Saunders's house filled with clowns…it all blurred together in one big chunk of time.

"It's more than spiders now," she said. "It's getting really bad."

"A serial killer?" Rose asked, sounding a little too interested.

"I think I liked it better when you were quiet," Avery said.

"So…a serial killer," Rose said, grinning at her mother's irritation. "One of those bad TV shows would stall and stall until the end and then come up with these profound ideas. That or some serious deus ex machina—a clue coming out of nowhere to save the day."

"Yeah, it rarely works that way in real life," Avery said. "In real life, it's honestly more like a game of Clue or Guess Who. It's sometimes less about clues and more about digging deeper into people's lives and their connections to suspected killers or other victims."

"Did your time off slow you down?" Rose asked.

"Maybe. I do feel a little off. And *damn,* I'm tired."

"I say we have a sleepover. Not to brag, but I can hook us up with some pretty righteous Jell-O."

"The sleepover sounds good," Avery said. "The Jello-O does not."

"Awesome. Pull your chair up and watch some TV with me."

"What are we watching?"

"Twenty women get catty with each other and cry about everything because some guy doesn't have enough roses for them."

And like that, something felt natural and almost repaired about their relationship. It was more than sweeping the past under the rug and pretending nothing had happened. It felt more like something had been *renewed.* And with renewal came the reality that they'd need to work on things but, as they worked together, they could learn to trust one another again.

Despite this, Avery drifted off to sleep fifteen minutes after moving her chair closer to Rose's bed so she could watch

135

television. She went to sleep with her own comments drifting around in her head like flotsam and jetsam.

It's sometimes less about clues and more about digging deeper into people's lives and their connections to suspected killers or other victims...

Avery didn't realize she had drifted off until her cell phone buzzed. It was in her pants pocket, so when it vibrated it woke her up with a start. Startled, Avery checked the phone. The first thing she saw was that it was 3:05 in the morning. The second thing she saw was that the buzzing had been an incoming text from Kellaway.

All of Dan Hudson's alibis check out. The one for Abby Costello isn't rock solid but it's enough to be considered verifiable given that he's been ruled out for killing Lawnbrook and Saunders. He meets with a lawyer tomorrow to represent him in the case that's currently being process in regards to him shooting you.

Avery then checked through her emails but found no new information on the case. She tried to drift back off to sleep but couldn't. She went to the bathroom and splashed some water in her face. When she came back out, Rose was awake.

"I heard your phone buzz. Are you off to save the city?"

"Not quite," Avery said. "But if you don't mind, I *am* going to go home and grab a shower before heading back to the precinct. Will you have someone call me when they release you? I'll come by and pick you up."

"You don't have to do that."

"Yes, I do. I want to. You've made a promise to yourself to stop hating me. The least I can do is make a promise to you that you'll be my top priority."

"I appreciate that, Mom," Rose said. "But can you start that *after* you bring this guy in? Seeing you struggle between me and a case is heartbreaking. And I know how you can get when you're knee-deep in a case. Go be a badass."

"If you say so," Avery said. "But I mean it...call me. I want to pick you up and take you home."

"Maybe I can come see your creepy little cabin in the woods when this is all over."

"I'd actually love that."

Avery gave Rose a kiss on the forehead and then headed back out. She again found herself thinking of connections and the members of the support group. There was something there, maybe something she needed to dig deeper into. She figured when morning arrived, she'd call Delores Moon and try to sort it all out.

She left the streetlights and buildings of the city and ventured out toward her new home. Things with Rose seemed to be better than ever and she also felt that she had something in her mind that she was on the verge of cracking into in regards to the case. The sun had another hour or so before it made its presence known but as for Avery, she already felt like today was going to be a good one.

***

Maybe it was having spent the last two days dealing with people and their fears, but Avery found it hard to be alone in the cabin when she arrived home. She felt like a foolish child, but she turned on just about every light in the house and turned the television on to a news channel just to have some active noise in the background. Hearing the murmur of the newscasters' voices made her feel oddly safe as she stripped down and took a shower.

She thought about what she'd said at Rose's bedside, about how there had to be some connection to the victims. But so far, the support group and Dan Hudson was the only link. Sure, fear itself was a link but their phobias had been so vastly different. So where was the connection? If she went deeper than just the support group itself, there was Delores Moon, but no red flags had gone off when Avery had met her. She wondered who else might have worked with the group in the past: other counselors, guest speakers, or anyone of that nature.

When she was out of the shower and dressed, she put on a pot of coffee. It was 5:05 when she scrambled some eggs and sliced up an avocado for breakfast. While she ate and drank her coffee, she Googled Delores Moon and came up with some pretty impressive results. She'd worked in a clinical supervision role for troubled teens and their families straight out of college before opening her own practice at the age of thirty-five. She'd been doing that for twelve years now, often volunteering her time to lead and manage small-group environments.

When she returned to the A1, she thought she might tackle some research to look into the fear support group to see if there had been anyone else involved with it recently. She worked a plan out in her mind as she put her dishes away and tidied up the house. She went outside, checked the mail, and swept the sidewalk, simply passing the time before Rose would call and ask to be picked up from the hospital.

Back inside, she sorted through the last two days' worth of mail, passing by bills and a flier for a furniture store sale. And behind that flier was letter with only her address. There was no return address. She recognized the handwriting at once.

Who are you, Avery?

She tore the envelope open right away. A sheet of notebook paper sat inside, folded perfectly into thirds. She unfolded it and found another of Howard's brief letters.

We all dwell on what we fear the most, he had written in an obnoxiously neat handwriting. *Whether spiders or losing your family, fear is the same in all its shapes. It is up to us if we let it control us, though. We all dwell on what we fear the most.*

She read it three times, noting right away that the opening line and the last line were the same. He was repeating it on purpose. It was really no different than sitting across that table in a back room in the prison, hoping he could lead her to some profound breakthrough that would crack a case. Despite the last three months, he was somehow still looking over her shoulder.

At least with the package that had arrived on the day she'd nearly killed herself, she could brush it off as Howard being eccentric.

Who are you, Avery? It was really a very deep and nonsensical sort of question.

But this letter was different. It seemed more purposeful. *We all dwell on what we fear the most.*

When her cell phone rang, she shook violently. *It's him,* she thought. *It's Howard calling...*

But the name and number on her phone's screen proved this paranoid theory wrong. It was Finley. And he was calling at 5:40 in the morning, which meant one of two things: either there was a break in the case or there was another victim.

"What have you got, Finley?"

"Nice to hear your voice, too," he joked. "Look...we're pulling at any straws we get here. We got a call twenty minutes ago from a guy named Joe Potter. He said he was worried about a friend of his. Said he got a weird call from his friend's cell phone. Jumbled noises and the sound of her crying."

"Maybe it was a butt dial?" Avery asked.

"Even if it was...the call came at four thirty in the morning. He tried calling back and it goes straight to voicemail. I'm calling you because of where the guy says he met his friend—a woman he made sure not to call his girlfriend."

"Where?" Avery asked.

"At a support group for phobias."

"Holy shit," Avery said. "Give me his number, would you?"

138

"I'll text it to you when we end this call. You want me to come out and lend a hand on this?"

"No, I think I'll keep Kellaway. But thanks all the same."

She ended the call and dialed up Kellaway. As she spoke to her new partner, she heard a tone in her ear as Finley's text came through. She set up plans with Kellaway and then placed another call, this one to Delores Moon.

She was in such a frenzy and preoccupied with the phone that on the way out of the cabin, she barely had time to pass a second glance at the letter she had received from Howard. Still, that one line remained plastered to the front of her mind as she got into her car and headed back into town.

We all dwell on what we fear the most...

CHAPTER THIRTY

Avery's call to Delores Moon had gone to voicemail. She'd left a message and then followed with a text: *Contact me ASAP. Potentially urgent.* Without her red strobe siren—an attachment that she'd started to use, the very same emergency light that Ramirez had always referred to as the Red Bubble—she realized she'd draw the attention of any cops in the area. She ran red lights and broke the speed limit all the way back into the city. And once again, she was able to recall how much she had loved the thrill of pursuit once upon a time.

When she pulled into the parking lot of Kellaway's apartment building, Avery's phone rang. She saw Kellaway standing on her stoop, waiting for her, and flashed her headlights at her. Dawn was on its way but had not yet done enough to eliminate the need for headlights.

Avery answered the phone, recognizing the number she had called less than twenty minutes ago.

"Detective Black?" Delores Moon asked. "I got your messages."

"Yes, and I'm sorry to have called you so early," she said. She then recounted what Finley had told her about Joe Potter's phone call. Before she was even done, Moon let out an audible gasp on the other line.

"The call was most likely from a woman named Heather Ellis. She was one of the dropouts you heard about yesterday. She stopped coming about a month or so ago because she and Joe had gotten somewhat romantic behind the scenes and their romance was distracting the rest of the group."

"Did she leave on good terms?" Avery asked.

"Oh yes. Heather had come a long way. She understood that Joe still needed the help of the group. She stopped coming willingly, though I had recommended her to some other resources."

"So she came to the small group with a phobia she was trying to overcome?"

"Yes indeed. A rather nasty fear of heights."

Kellaway reached the car and stepped inside. When she saw Avery on the phone she stayed quiet. Avery put the call on speakerphone and set it on the console.

140

"Had she overcome that fear while in the group?" Avery asked.

"She'd gotten a bit better. But the fear of heights is so common that it is rarely taken seriously."

"And what about Joe Potter? What is his fear?"

"He's actually one of the men that was present when you came to the meeting—the gentleman that was afraid of the very idea of death. I think he and Heather had hoped that their relationship might help in getting over their fears."

"And has Joe ever shown any reason for you to maybe find him violent or in any way suspicious?"

"Not at all."

"I do have one more question for you," Avery said. "How long, exactly, have you been leading the group we attended yesterday?"

"Seven months," she answered. "Though I've led countless other small groups just like it over the last five years or so."

"And was there a preexisting position for it when you started with this group, or was it one of your own making?"

"There was a counselor who had been operating it for about a year or so before me, I believe. A nice albeit cocky gentleman named Barry Kechner. He was more in favor of a tough love approach than I am."

"Do you know why he left?"

"I never spoke with him about it," Moon said. "In fact, out paths only ever crossed once during the transition process. A few of the group members that were around when he was there claim that he was often short on patience."

"Do you know where he might be now?" Avery asked.

"No idea. Actually, I can't recall the last time I heard his name. If I remember correctly, he had worked as a counselor at a rehabilitation facility somewhere in the city for a few years. He may have gone back to that."

"Thanks for the information," Avery said. "Please…would you mind another call should I need more information?"

"Of course…whatever I can do to help."

Avery ended the call and looked over at Kellaway. "Sorry for the early start to the day, but things suddenly just got a lot more interesting."

"I gathered that. Where to now?"

It was a good question. While the initial call about Heather Ellis had come from Joe Potter, Avery didn't think paying him an immediate visit would be worthwhile—especially not if there was a chance that Heather *was* in trouble and might still be out there, alive somewhere.

141

Maybe being tortured via her fear, Avery thought.

Avery picked her phone back up, calling up Finley. He answered right away with a tone of sleepiness but his usual good cheer. "What can I do for you, Avery?"

"I need you to get a team ready for me. A few, maybe. I need someone to pull anything and everything we might have on file for a man named Barry Kechner. I need that done right away. I also need you to send me the address for Heather Ellis; that's apparently Joe Potter's girlfriend."

"The potential butt-dial?" Finley said.

"It's looking that way. If the call *did* come from Heather's cell and she's the killer's next potential victim, I think a visit to *her* place might be worth more than trying to talk to Joe Potter. That being said, I think someone *should* go visit with him just to make sure he isn't sitting on some information."

"Got it. And this Kechner guy...who is he?"

"I'm not sure yet," Avery said. "Maybe our killer. But keep that quiet until you know if he's even in the system. Thanks, Finley. Just get me an address for Heather Ellis as soon as you can."

"You'll have it within five minutes."

When Avery ended the call, the silence in the car seemed to have a weight to it. To break it, Avery filled Kellaway in on the bits she had missed.

"So you think this Barry Kechner might be the guy?" Kellaway asked.

"I don't know," Avery said. "Based on the things Moon told me, it *feels* right. If that makes sense."

"Good old police intuition?" Kellaway asked.

"Something like that."

As it turned out, Avery didn't even have to wait five minutes. Her phone rang again before three minutes had passed. This time, she was surprised to see that it was a line coming from the A1 rather than Finley's cell.

"Finley?"

"No, this is Connelly. I just happened to be passing by Finley's office when he got this information on Barry Kechner for you. Avery...I think this might be it. There's a record here that's not very long but hints at some bad stuff. There's a cruelty to animals charge from way back twenty years ago. And there's a restraining order against him, placed by an old coworker from when he worked at Center Field Rehab Center."

"Got an address? Kellaway and I can head over there right now."

142

"Yeah, I've got it. And I think me and Finley will meet you over there, too. If this is our guy and he might have the next victim, there's no sense in taking chances."

While she hated the idea of Connelly out on the scene, she knew it was pointless to argue it. She couldn't help but wonder if this was his way of making sure she was still operating at full capacity. Maybe he wanted to see for himself if the last few months had made her rusty.

He gave her the address and Kellaway put it into her phone. "We can be there in about ten minutes," Avery said.

"You'll beat us by a few," Connelly said. "Don't do anything until we get there."

She hung up before responding. It was just a habit that she apparently had not grown out of. And so what if it pissed him off? What was he going to do...fire her?

With an address and a potential suspect ten minutes away, the sun finally started to paint the first rays of gold across the horizon. The city was just now starting to wake up as Avery sped ahead of morning traffic.

It might have been the first time she'd felt *truly* alive since she'd watched Ramirez's casket lowered into the ground.

CHAPTER THIRTY ONE

Avery and Kellaway did indeed arrive at Barry Kechner's residence before Connelly and Finley. She didn't get there much sooner, though; she could already see the glare of headlights coming around the corner behind them, likely a single car occupied by Connelly and Finley. The house itself was located in the cul de sac of a side street off to the edge of an upper-class neighborhood. The porch light was on and the garage was closed, making it impossible to tell if anyone was home.

"You ready?" Avery asked.

Kellaway nodded, looking to the house. "You don't know much about me," Kellaway said. "So now might be a good time to let you know that when I was in New York, I had to fire my weapon for the very first time in a situation like this."

"Self-defense?"

"Yeah. My shot went low, though. I was going for the shoulder and somehow ended up clipping him at the top of the lung. He survived, but it was bad."

"You getting the jitters?" Avery asked.

"No, just some bad memories. I'll be fine."

The headlights that had been approaching from behind settled to a stop behind them. The doors to the car opened right away as Connelly and Finley stepped out. Avery and Kellaway joined them and for a moment, they stood in front of the house. The first true light of dawn etched their shadows along Kechner's sidewalk, as if pushing them forward.

They hurried to the front door quietly. Connelly took the lead, ringing the doorbell. When there was no answer after ten seconds, he rang again and followed it with a hefty knock on the door. His response was more silence.

"You think there's enough probable cause for us to storm in anyway?" Avery asked. If it were up to her, she'd break in without question. But with Connelly here, things were different. It was one of the reasons she hadn't wanted him to come along.

"I honestly don't know," Connelly said. "But given that we have a fourth probable victim and this guy seems to be our one solid lead, I'll allow it."

144

As he said this, Connelly stepped forward again. He pulled a snap gun out of his pocket, something Avery would have never expected. It was shaped like a small gun, a device used to open just about any pin tumbler lock. She'd used them many times before but had assumed it would be too controversial for Connelly. She watched as Connelly inserted the thin steel rod into the lock and then engaged it against all of the pins within the lock. There was a very loud click noise as the lock was disengaged.

Avery quickly drew her Glock, pushed the door open, and swung around inside the doorframe. As the other three fell in behind her, she took in her surroundings. It was a very nice house, the front door leading into a large foyer. From the foyer, there was a split to the house; left to head into what looked like a den and right, which led to a study and a hallway beyond. The study was dimly lit with a desk lamp, providing a slight glow for them to see by.

Without saying a word, protocol kicked in. Avery and Kellaway went into the study while Connelly and Finley checked the den area and the darkened spaces beyond. When Avery spotted the closed laptop on the desk, she went to it right away. She opened it up and found it locked at a password screen.

She barely had time to feel frustration at this before she saw the thin stack of papers to the right of the laptop. One was a sketch of what looked like a rough map. On one edge of it was a wobbly circle. The letters *JP* were in the center of it.

Beneath this sketch was a torn sheet of paper with a few words scrawled on it. Every single one sent a chill directly into her heart. "You see this?" Avery asked over her shoulder to Kellaway.

"Yeah…"

The words on the paper read: *tarantula? Black widow? Funnel web (atrax robustus)?* There were a few other spiders written down but they were all crossed out. There were also several company names and three websites written down. One of the websites was one that she had visited while doing her digging on Stefon Scott.

Beneath this list there was a stapled grouping of papers. They all looked to be printouts and receipts. She scanned them quickly and saw the word *clown* or *doll* pop up quite frequently.

She then looked back to the rough map. She looked at the circle labeled *JP* and saw several little Xs marked around the edge of it. *JP,* she thought. *Jamaica Pond. And I bet each of those Xs is a potential dumping point…*

"It's him," Avery said. "I don't see anything that might pinpoint Heather Ellis, but the other three…it's clearly him. We have to—"

145

She was interrupted by Connelly's voice, a loud mutter that crept through the house. *"What the actual FUCK?"*

Avery ran to the den, following the direction of Connelly's voice. Kellaway trailed behind her, having drawn her weapon. The den emptied off into a large hallway that seemed to wrap around to meet the hallway off of the study. Before that turn, though, there were several rooms. Two of these doors were open. Sounds of disgust could be heard coming from one of them as Finley came slowly stepping out. His back was turned to Avery as he continued to face inside the room. "Get out," he said, apparently to Connelly. "What the hell are you doing?"

"What is it?" Avery asked.

Finley looked like he had seen a ghost when he turned around to face Avery. "I don't even know. It looks like Kechner was doing some research and it got away from him."

Avery hurried to the door and was not at all prepared for what she saw. She had to pause in the doorway for a moment to give herself time to adjust.

Connelly was standing just a few feet away from her. He, too, looked frozen. He was looking into the far corner where a glass case sat on the floor—a glass case very similar to the one she had seen in Stefon Scott's apartment. Most of the glass had been covered by the thin filaments of spider webs. But the webs had not been contained to the case. They were on the walls as well, thin strands that led to wider and intricately woven webs in the corners up near the ceiling.

And there were spiders everywhere. *Big* spiders. Some were crawling along the walls while others scurried on the floor.

"You think he did this on purpose?" Connelly asked.

"I don't know," Avery said, slowly backing out, unable to take her eyes away from the spiders. "Maybe. Maybe he was breeding them."

None of the spiders she saw was smaller than a penny. Some, she thought, might be able to *swallow* a penny. The idea that some of these may be the funnel web spiders crossed her mind and she backed out a little faster.

"Come on," she said. "I've got enough proof in the study that Kechner is our guy. We need to haul ass and find him before we get a call about someone discovering Heather Ellis's corpse."

"Yeah, good idea," Connelly said. Whatever fugue had overcome him seemed to slip away as he turned toward the door.

Avery waited for him to come out, wanting to bring up the rear in the event Kechner *was* actually home and just waiting to jump out and ambush them. And it was because she took up the rear that

146

she saw the spider crawling up the back of Connelly's shirt. It was a large one, but not abnormally large. The coloring was odd and looked familiar; she'd seen a spider like that recently, while doing research.

Funnel web spider...

She opened her mouth to say something but in that moment, the spider had reached the bare skin of Connelly's neck. Feeling it there, he instinctively swatted at it. In one moment, the house was filled with the sound of Connelly slapping at his neck and the next, it was filled with him howling in pain.

It was more like a roar, actually. He slapped furiously at his neck again and fell against the wall. Avery looked to the dimly lit hallway floor and saw the spider scurrying away. Working on her own instinct, Avery lifted her foot and slammed it down on the creature. There was a satisfying crunch under her heel.

Finley went to Connelly's side, checking the area. No longer worried about stealth, Avery flipped the nearest light switch, filling the hallway with the light. The first thing she saw was the bite on Connelly's neck. It was already growing red and swollen. The second thing she saw was two spiders coming out of the room which they had neglected to close—not that it would have mattered, because the smaller ones could have easily crept under the closed door. It made her wonder how many were already out in the house, wandering around and within inches of her own exposed skin.

She helped Finley get Connelly to his feet while Kellaway grabbed her phone and called for an ambulance. Back out in the open air, Avery felt a bit better, no longer feeling herself freak out about potential spiders descending on her.

"How much trouble am I in?" Connelly asked through a hiss of pain as they carried him back out to the cars.

"The truth or comfort?" Avery asked.

"Truth."

"I'm pretty sure it was a funnel web spider that got you. Several of their bites is what killed Alfred Lawnbrook. Depending on the species, you'll be dead within an hour or just really sick for a few days."

"Shit," Connelly said.

"An ambulance is on the way," Kellaway announced, pocketing her phone. "ETA eleven minutes."

"Do you want us to just drive you?" Finley asked. "It might be faster in the long run."

"Bad idea," Avery said. "If there's venom involved, he's going to need drugs ASAP. I imagine they'll administer them to him the moment they get here."

"She's right," Connelly said. He had fallen into the passenger seat of his car. He was starting to tremble a bit and the bite itself was getting nastier by the moment.

"Black...Kellaway...go get this asshole. Do whatever you need to do. Just get him and bring his ass to the A1."

Avery hated to leave Connelly while in this state but knew that he was in capable hands with Finley. She gave Finley a stern look, trying her best to hide her concern for what was looking to be a rather grave situation.

"Keep me posted on his status," she said.

"You got it. Now go do what you do."

Avery and Kellaway hurried to their car with Avery now more determined than ever. Barry Kechner was certainly not aware of it at this early hour, but he had just inadvertently hurt someone she respected and admired. Depending on how quickly Connelly got treatment, he could end up worse than just *hurt*.

"Pull up Heather Ellis's address," Avery told Kellaway. "I think that's our next stop."

"What do you think we'll find?"

"I'm not sure," she said. She then recited the line from Howard's latest letter, hoping that it was also true of Heather Ellis and could help them save her before it was too late. "Because we dwell on what we fear the most."

148

CHAPTER THIRTY TWO

Avery was not at all surprised to find that Heather Ellis was not at home. She lived in an apartment in a three-story building. When Avery and Kellaway arrived, people had started to wake up and get ready for their days. Some were even heading out of the door, perhaps hoping to get to work a little early. It was a reminder to Avery that sometime in the next few hours she should be getting a call from Rose, asking her to come pick her up from the hospital.

And if this case keeps going on all cylinders like this, Avery thought, *I won't be able to make it. Dammit...*

The door to the apartment was not locked. And being that there was no one home and the woman that lived here was suspected missing or abducted, that was an automatic red flag to Avery.

Inside, Heather's apartment was a cute little space that looked like something off of a minimalist's blog. And because it was so well kept and tidy, it was easy to see the signs of a recent struggle. A glass vase had been toppled from the small coffee table; it had not shattered but had fallen securely on the plush rug under the table. A pair of bedroom slippers was scattered across the living room, one by the front door and one beside the little counter that ran along the course of the kitchen.

A laptop sat on a small decorative desk on the other side of the living room. While it was password protected, there was a picture on the lock screen that perhaps proved that Heather Ellis was indeed trying to overcome her fear. It showed a shirtless man with shaggy hair cliff diving off of some picturesque cliff. The production quality of the picture told Avery that it was not a personal picture, but one Heather had likely found online somewhere.

They checked the rest of the apartment for any indication of where Barry Kechner might have taken her. She seriously doubted that he'd take her to some exotic location to go cliff diving and Boston didn't really offer such attractions.

In Heather's bedroom, there was a small drawing desk where several sketches and impressive pastel drawings had been done. She saw meadows and trees done in pastel, as well as what looked like a woman in a dress, from the waist down. One of the drawings was a very well-done representation of a bridge, partially obscured by fog and mist. Over the desk was a frame made of pallet board with

149

scarred wood on the inside. Within the frame was a quote, done in an elegant and trendy type of lettering.

The quote read:

I must not fear. Fear is the mind-killer. Fear is the little-death that brings total obliteration. I will face my fear. I will permit it to pass over me and through me. And when it has gone past I will turn the inner eye to see its path. Where the fear has gone there will be nothing. Only I will remain.
– Frank Herbert

"That bridge," Kellaway said, nodding to the pastel drawing. "You know what it is, right?"

Avery looked back to it and realized that she did know what it was. She'd thought it looked familiar the first time she had looked at it but had been too busy looking for something a little more obvious.

"Tobin Bridge," she said. And on the heels of that, Howard again: *We dwell on what we fear the most.*

"That's the tallest bridge in the city, right?" Kellaway asked.

"And Heather Ellis is afraid of heights."

Before the last comment was out of her mouth, Avery pulled out her phone. With Finley and Connelly out of commission for the time being, she pulled up O'Malley's number.

"Hey, Black," O'Malley said. "Why did you not call me about Connelly before now? He's going to—"

"O'Malley, I need you to reach out to the city and get a shitload of people together right now. We have to close down Tobin Bridge."

"What? Are you insane?"

Avery and Kellaway were already out of Heather's apartment and heading back down the stairs. Avery's voice jostled a bit with each stair she took. "I can almost guarantee you that's where the killer has taken his latest victim, Heather Ellis. I don't know how long he holds on to them before he kills them, but maybe…"

"Maybe there's a chance," O'Malley said. "You sure about this, Black?"

"Just do it," she nearly snapped into the phone.

When they were back in their car, Avery peeled out into morning traffic, beeping her horn at the starting surge of morning traffic.

"You think she's still alive?" Kellaway asked.

Avery thought of Lawnbrook, killed by spiders. Of Abby Costello, tossed into a secluded section of Jamaica Pond, and of

Janice Saunders, terrified of the clowns that had abruptly showed up in her house. Each of those scenes had taken dedication and time to set up. She wondered how long Kechner had stood there and watched Abby Costello frantically trying to swim to the surface...how long he had stabbed Janice Saunders while he enjoyed her terror.

Someone like this...he might take his time. He might want to prolong things as long as he could.

"I think she might be," Avery said.

And while it was a very faint hope, it was at least something to cling to as she weaved through traffic toward the Tobin Bridge.

CHAPTER THIRTY THREE

The Tobin Bridge housed six lanes of US Highway 1 and crossed over Mystic River. It was a double-deck truss bridge that sat a little more than two hundred and fifty feet over the water at its highest point. As the bridge came into view, Avery was pretty sure that anyone trying to remain at least somewhat private in their actions would stay away from the middle of the bridge where morning traffic would be at its thickest.

She knew that the deck beneath the bridge would be the most probable location for Barry Kechner to do his demented work. Doing it off of the upper deck where traffic zoomed by in the morning would be opening himself up to being caught easily. On the lower deck, he'd only have joggers and pedestrians to worry about. And given the cold weather, she doubted there would be many people out for a run or walk on the bridge this early.

It was 7:56 when she and Kellaway arrived at the Tobin Bridge. Before she was even out of the car, she saw O'Malley shouting instructions at a team of other officers and a crew from the Massachusetts Department of Transportation. They were working feverishly to block off traffic from the bridge and doing so in a way that was as subtle and non-obstructive as possible. It was a smart move; if Barry Kechner was indeed here with Heather Ellis, there was no sense in tipping him off in any way.

Avery and Kellaway rushed over to O'Malley. A look of relief flashed across his face when he saw her. When he spoke, his voice was hoarse from all of the shouting he'd been doing to be heard over the roar of morning traffic coming on and off of the Tobin Bridge.

"Any sign of him?" Avery asked.

"Yes, in fact. Two different drivers coming off of the bridge have stopped to tell us that there was a man walking along the edge, right between the rails. He had a woman with him that looked like she did not want to be with him. Seems to have been sighted just before the toll plaza. His car is pulled as far to the side as it will go. Dumbass even put his hazard lights on."

"How long ago?" Avery asked, her heart now slamming in her chest.

"I don't know," O'Malley said, looking at his watch. "Maybe seven minutes ago?"

152

"Okay," Avery said. "Let us in."

She went back to her car and impatiently waited for O'Malley and his team to make way for her to enter the bridge.

"So he's here?" Kellaway asked.

"Seems like it," Avery said as she sped through the narrow lane O'Malley had made for her.

She picked up speed quickly, heading for the toll plaza and Chelsea, waiting on the other side. The cleared lanes helped immensely and by the time her speed had reached fifty, she saw the car pulled over to the side of the bridge in what served as a thin breakdown lane, a pad of sorts along the edge of the bridge allowing for problematic or stranded motorists. Sure enough, she saw someone standing on the other side of the protective cables. The figure looked abnormal but that was only because it was actually *two* bodies: Barry Kechner and Heather Ellis.

"You good?" Avery asked, reaching for her door handle.

Kellaway nodded as she opened her door and instantly went for her Glock. She did not pull it but kept her hand resting there, light and ready to move at a moment's notice. Avery felt her muscles twitching to do the same but she knew it would be a mistake. If she was taking the lead on this, Kechner could not see her in any sort of defensive position.

When they stepped onto the pavement, the bridge was eerily quiet. Kechner and Heather Ellis stood about ten yards ahead of them, both clinging to the rails at the far edge of the bridge. The drop to the Mystic River below might not kill her, but it would probably hurt her enough to make it impossible to swim to shore. Avery looked to their hands, both clinging to the rails. One sudden movement or even just a sweaty palm, and they'd both go falling in an instant.

Avery walked slowly. She could feel Kellaway behind her like some weird gravity that kept her grounded.

"Barry Kechner?" Avery asked. She didn't shout, but raised her voice enough to sound as if it were booming across the quiet bridge. The chilled air carried it to Kechner, who had already turned in their direction at the sound of their engine coming to a stop behind his car.

"We're fine here," he said. His voice sounded soft and almost pleasant. He might have been anyone out for a morning stroll.

"Who is that you have with you?" Avery asked. When the question was out of her mouth, she took two more steps forward. He was now about six yards away, the rails between them. Another few steps and she'd be able to reach out and grab Heather Ellis.

153

Avery could just barely see Heather. She was wearing a hoodie, the hood pulled up. All Avery could see of her was one brown eye, curly brown hair spilling outside of the hood, and a sharp pointed nose.

"Just a friend," Kechner said. "I'm helping her. We'll be done in a minute."

"Well, you see, you've parked your car on the side of the bridge. And it's technically illegal for you to be standing over there on the other side of the rails. Not to mention…it's very dangerous. You need to come back over here to the pavement, okay?"

Kechner looked at her with an almost childlike expression. He was looking at her as if he thought she was an idiot. She guessed him to be about fifty-five, maybe pushing sixty. He wore a stocking cap, a puffy black coat, and work boots that were planted firmly on the lower rail, the toes hanging out over empty space.

Kellaway came up beside Avery and gave her a questioning look. *You mind?* that look seemed to ask. Avery gave a quick, curt nod and Kellaway slowly stepped forward. She did not look nervous but she was certainly a far cry from confident.

"Mr. Kechner, why have you brought Heather here?" Kellaway asked. As she spoke, she took a small baby step forward and then another—both so small and seemingly insignificant that it appeared as if she had hardly moved.

"She wants to be here. She—"

"NO!" Heather Ellis screamed. "No I don't! Please help me!"

At the interruption, Kechner placed his hand on Heather's. For only split second, his hand had been free, his body perched over the water by only leaning against the rail. Avery thought if a strong wind came by, it might have thrown him off balance just enough to send them both plunging over, two hundred and fifty feet to the frigid water below.

Again, Kellaway took another baby step and then one daring large one. She had closed to within less than five yards of them now. Avery took another step forward as well and slightly to the right. If they could end up bookending Kechner and Heather, they might get out of this without anyone dying.

"Step forward one more time," Kechner said, "and I'll push her. I'd be doing her a favor, you know? She needs to be over this fear."

"Maybe you're right," Avery said. "But look…your car is still blocking the lane and we need you to move it."

154

"I'm not stupid," Kechner said. "I know why you're here. I suppose you know about Lawnbrook, Costello, and Saunders, too. Don't you? You want to arrest me?"

"I don't know," Avery said. "We'll have to talk it all out and see."

He knows I'm lying, she thought. *He knows he's in serious trouble and that makes him all the more dangerous.*

"No talking," he said. "She'll be my last. And I'll go with her."

He turned and looked at them and Avery saw not a single flicker of fear. He truly thought he was helping his victims, perhaps taking them out of a world where their fear controlled them.

Several things happened in the three seconds that followed; it all felt as if it were in slow motion but the weight of it made it also feel fluid and uncontrollable.

Kechner pounded his fist into Heather's hand and pushed her. Her body went tilting forward. She let out a scream, flailing for a rail that was too far away from her grasp. As she tottered forward, her body giving way to gravity, Kellaway launched herself toward the railing. In doing so, her right arm slammed into Kechner while her left reached out and grabbed Heather. She barely caught her, snagging her by the hood of her sweater. It stopped the forward momentum just enough for Kellaway to pull her backward. The sound of the fabric of her hoodie tearing was impossibly loud.

As Heather grasped the rail again, Kechner drew his fist back and caught Kellaway in the side of the face. She stumbled back and when she did, Kechner grabbed her right arm and pulled it hard toward him. Kellaway was again slammed into the railing, letting out a groan of pain.

Avery opted not to draw her Glock, feeling that she'd need both hands as she dashed forward. By the time she got to the rail, Kechner had grabbed Kellaway by the hair and chin, hauling her over the rail. The moment Avery reached them, Kellaway's feet were in the air as she toppled over the rail. She screamed as her body went flailing toward the water.

Avery screamed and applied a headlock on Kechner from behind the rail. He struggled against her but she tightened her grip, choking him out. The leverage of the rail between them worked to his advantage, though. He pressed against it, pulling her closer to him.

"Heather, can you crawl over?" she said, hissing through her effort of keeping Kechner immobile.

But Heather was paralyzed, starting down at the water. Avery followed her gaze and saw something that made her heart swell:

Kellaway, clinging to the bottom edge of the lower level of the bridge. The edge didn't allow much room for her to pull herself up, but she was carefully moving herself to the left, toward a thick cable that she could cling to and hopefully use to scale back up to the rails.

"O'Malley!" Avery screamed. "O'Malley, we need help!"

That moment of distraction was all Kechner needed. He slammed his head backward, the back of his skull connected solidly with Avery's mouth. She felt her lip burst and tasted blood right away. She released her grip and stumbled back.

This time, she acted quickly, not making the mistake of leaving her Glock holstered. She withdrew it and aimed right away.

Kechner was clasping Heather's wrist, trying to pull it away from the rail. Heather shook and trembled as one finger after the other was pried up.

"Let her go, Kechner," Avery bellowed. "Last warning!"

He didn't even give Avery the consideration of looking her way. He now had both hands on Heather, determined to pry her loose. It would mean that he would fall with her but compared to the time he'd spend in jail for four murders, Avery assumed he'd rather have death.

She could help him in that regard.

"Let her go!"

When he didn't respond this time, Avery took a step forward, aimed with skill that had remained with her during her time off, and squeezed the trigger.

In her career, she had avoided headshots at all costs. But this time, she had no choice. Anything other than a certain kill shot might only injure him, causing him to fall and take Heather with him.

The shot landed true, creating a black hole directly between Kechner's eyes. He looked almost confused for a moment as his body went limp. His hands unclenched themselves from Heather and he went falling backward.

Avery ran forward, relieved to see that his falling body had missed Kellaway by a good five feet. She had made it over to the cable and was using it to hoist herself upward, her feet inching along the side of the bridge back toward the rails.

As for Kechner, his body continued to fall. She watched it until it slammed into the cold water below them. Even Heather Ellis seemed to break out of her frozen state to watch his descent.

Kellaway was still out of her reach, about ten feet down along the edge of the bridge. She looked tired and nervous as hell.

156

"Can you make it?" Avery asked, looking for a way over to where she could help.

Kellaway only nodded, her attention solely on the cable and the edge of the bridge. Behind them, two cars pulled to a screeching stop as O'Malley and five officers arrived. They got out of the car with guns drawn.

"Barry Kechner is dead," Avery said. "And Kellaway is hanging on for dear life over here!"

By the time O'Malley and the others had reached the rail, Kellaway had firm footing on the same ledge that Heather Ellis was perched on. She slowly made her way over to her, holding on to the rail for dear life.

"Heather," she said. "Come on back to the other side with me, what do you say?"

Heather nodded and said something, but Avery didn't hear it.

Her phone was ringing. She checked it quickly and saw that it was Rose.

Shit, Avery thought. *I'm supposed to pick her up from the hosp...*

The thought seemed to fracture and break as the world grew dizzy. She looked to Kellaway, slowly helping Heather back over the rail and to the pavement on the other side. Avery smiled wanly, took a stumbling step forward, and then passed out.

CHAPTER THIRTY FOUR

Three days later, Avery found herself sitting in Connelly's office. It was Connelly's first day back, having mostly recovered from the spider bite. It had been a weaker genus of funnel web spider and though its venom was still deadly, it had been stalled by several injections at the hospital. Connelly still wore a small bandage over the area where he had been bitten but other than that, he was basically back to his old self.

And that included a brash and transparent communication approach. He looked over his desk at Avery and sighed. It was just the two of them and the door was closed. It felt both intimate and suffocating all at once.

"I want you back," he said. "I know you've been through hell and this Barry Kechner case was only a favor you did for the Al but...I want you back. I want you working for me until you're too old to hold up a gun."

Avery couldn't help but smile at the thought of a fifty-five-year-old version of herself battling with Barry Kechner on the edge of the Tobin Bridge.

"I appreciate that," Avery said. "And I'd be lying if I told you that I had absolutely no interest in coming back for a few more years. But for right now—in the next few weeks or months—I have to focus on Rose. I have to get my personal life right before I can think about my work."

The right side of her head was still sore from the fall she'd taken on the bridge. While the doctors who had seen to her had no real reason why she had passed out, the psychiatrist she'd seen yesterday seemed to think it was some sort of emotional or mental trauma—that her old life and desires were crashing into the need to correct things with her family. Her mind had felt exhausted for a moment and had simply shut itself down for a moment. It had been enough motivation for her to choose one over the other as she sorted her life out, and Rose had won out without much of a contest.

Connelly nodded and relaxed in his seat. "I can respect that. I expected it, even. So...do I need to let Finley know he only has your office for a few more weeks?"

"No," she said with another smile. "Let him keep it. And please...Connelly, do me a favor?"

"What's that?"

"Wait for me to call you this time. I'll be back. I just…well, I have to finally put Rose first."

"Understood," Connelly said, getting to his feet. He went to the door and opened it for her. "Now get out of here before you see what I look like when I pout if I don't get my way."

Avery did as he asked. She thought about going to say goodbye to Finley and O'Malley but didn't want to draw any more attention to herself. She'd already been lauded a hero because of her actions on the bridge. Kellaway had also enjoyed some of the praise and was already back out on the streets working her next case. Avery couldn't wait to see what became of the young woman's career.

Hell, who knew…maybe someday soon, they'd share another case. Avery certainly hoped so; she was well aware that she still owed Kellaway for saving her life.

***

She had originally feared that having Rose around the cabin would be weird. But in the end, it turned out to be exactly what she needed…what they *both* needed, actually. The plan they'd come up with on their first night in the cabin together was to unplug from everything, to just stay in the cabin as winter approached and get to know one another again. If necessary, they'd talk about Jack, they'd talk about Ramirez, and how life had dealt them a shitty hand as of late.

Rose had also agreed to family therapy and although neither of them liked the idea, they were also not too stubborn to realize how much it could help them.

On her second week at the cabin, Rose sat down on the couch with Avery. Avery's reading habits had turned to fiction, something pointless and inane to just reset her mind, to keep the stress of the real world away.

"Hey, Mom?" Rose said. Her voice was soft and sweet, letting Avery know that what was coming was not going to be easy for Rose to say.

"Yeah?"

"I want to live here for a while," she said. "And not just to fix us. I mean into the foreseeable future. As I finish school, as I find an *actual* job."

"I think I'd like that, too," Avery said, her heart about to burst.

"I don't want to be the deadbeat kid that still lives with her mom, though. I want you to charge me rent. I want to be roommates."

159

"So long as you're my daughter first, that's fine with me."

Rose nodded and gave her mom a smile. Avery's heart ached a bit when she was reminded just now much of Jack peeked out when Rose smiled.

"Now, as my roommate," Avery said, "I do believe it is your turn to do the dishes."

"Oh, you're going to be *that* kind of roommate," Rose said with a smirk. Still, she got up from the couch and walked into the kitchen.

Avery looked out of the back window to the trees, now stripped completely. The sky looked like snow, though there was none in the forecast. She thought about the quiet hill somewhere out there she had once tried to hunt and realized that she did not quite recognize that woman any longer.

And that was fine. Because that woman had nearly given up, had thought about ending her own life. And quite frankly, Avery hated that bitch.

EPILOGUE

They fell into a routine easily enough. They started therapy, they shared the duties when it came to cooking meals, they went for walks in the cold, and they did indeed talk about the loved ones they had lost. When they were comfortable enough with their living arrangement, they "re-plugged" (a term Rose used to gear enthusiasm) and started watching TV together. It eerily *was* like she had a roommate. But every now and then they'd come to a tough topic in conversation or one of them would have a bad dream and they'd end up uncovering the mother-daughter relationship they had kept buried for so long.

Avery was thinking about this turn in their relationship on one of her runs around Walden Pond. It was the only time of the day she allowed herself to be alone. Sometimes her mind would wander toward work, but that was okay. She did miss it, but not with the same urgency as she had months before. She and Rose had been living together for six weeks now and Rose still held sway over work. Even though Rose had told her that it was okay for her to go back to work, Avery hesitated. She had to make sure she was fully prepared, fully invested.

The Barry Kechner case had caused quite a few nightmares and she still wondered if there might have been some way to keep Kellaway from nearly plummeting into the Mystic River—or even if there might have been some way to prevent putting a bullet between Kechner's eyes.

She saw him falling down into the river at least three times a day. That was an improvement, though; in the first week after the incident on the bridge, she'd replayed that moment at least a hundred times a day.

It was Kechner's falling body that was on her mind as she wrapped up her run. Her cabin came into view, her signal to slow her pace to a mild sprint. She dimly thought of Kellaway, thinking of calling her up to ask her if she'd like to come over for dinner with her and Rose one night. Maybe they could get to know one another better outside of work and—

Avery stopped as she reached her porch steps. There was a piece of paper sticking out from beneath the welcome mat at the front door. She walked up the stairs and approached it cautiously, as if it were one of Stefon Scott's spiders rather than a sheet of paper.

161

She plucked it out from beneath the mat and unfolded it. There were a few words written on it, words she read at least ten times before moving again.

what are you afraid of, avery?
   -HR

She finally folded the paper up and looked out toward the woods that surrounded her house. The quiet bore down on her as she stood on the porch, breathing hard from her run as a mild panic started to flare within her blood.

The other letters had unnerved her, sure. But this letter was different.

This letter had not been mailed.

This one was hand delivered.

Howard Randall had been to her house.

NOW AVAILABLE!

A TRACE OF DEATH
(A Keri Locke Mystery--Book #1)

"A dynamic story line that grips from the first chapter and doesn't let go."
--Midwest Book Review, Diane Donovan (regarding Once Gone)

From #1 bestselling mystery author Blake Pierce comes a new masterpiece of psychological suspense.

Keri Locke, Missing Persons Detective in the Homicide division of the LAPD, remains haunted by the abduction of her own daughter, years before, never found. Still obsessed with finding her, Keri buries her grief the only way she knows how: by throwing herself into the cases of missing persons in Los Angeles.

A routine phone call from a worried mother of a high-schooler, only two hours missing, should be ignored. Yet something about the mother's voice strikes a chord, and Keri decides to investigate.

What she finds shocks her. The missing daughter—of a prominent senator—was hiding secrets no one knew. When all evidence points to a runaway, Keri is ordered off the case. And yet, despite pressure from her superiors, from the media, despite all trails going cold, the brilliant and obsessed Keri refuses to let it go. She knows she has but 48 hours if she has any chance of bringing this girl back alive.

A dark psychological thriller with heart-pounding suspense, A TRACE OF DEATH marks the debut of a riveting new series—and a beloved new character—that will leave you turning pages late into the night.

"A masterpiece of thriller and mystery! The author did a magnificent job developing characters with a psychological side that is so well described that we feel inside their minds, follow their fears and cheer for their success. The plot is very intelligent and

will keep you entertained throughout the book. Full of twists, this book will keep you awake until the turn of the last page."
--Books and Movie Reviews, Roberto Mattos (re Once Gone)

Book #2 in the Keri Locke series is also now available!

Blake Pierce

Blake Pierce is author of the bestselling RILEY PAGE mystery series, which includes eleven books (and counting). Blake Pierce is also the author of the MACKENZIE WHITE mystery series, comprising seven books (and counting); of the AVERY BLACK mystery series, comprising six books; and of the new KERI LOCKE mystery series, comprising four books (and counting).

An avid reader and lifelong fan of the mystery and thriller genres, Blake loves to hear from you, so please feel free to visit www.blakepierceauthor.com to learn more and stay in touch.

BOOKS BY BLAKE PIERCE

RILEY PAIGE MYSTERY SERIES
ONCE GONE (Book #1)
ONCE TAKEN (Book #2)
ONCE CRAVED (Book #3)
ONCE LURED (Book #4)
ONCE HUNTED (Book #5)
ONCE PINED (Book #6)
ONCE FORSAKEN (Book #7)
ONCE COLD (Book #8)
ONCE STALKED (Book #9)
ONCE LOST (Book #10)
ONCE BURIED (Book #11)
ONCE BOUND (Book #12)

MACKENZIE WHITE MYSTERY SERIES
BEFORE HE KILLS (Book #1)
BEFORE HE SEES (Book #2)
BEFORE HE COVETS (Book #3)
BEFORE HE TAKES (Book #4)
BEFORE HE NEEDS (Book #5)
BEFORE HE FEELS (Book #6)
BEFORE HE SINS (Book #7)
BEFORE HE HUNTS (Book #8)

AVERY BLACK MYSTERY SERIES
CAUSE TO KILL (Book #1)
CAUSE TO RUN (Book #2)
CAUSE TO HIDE (Book #3)
CAUSE TO FEAR (Book #4)
CAUSE TO SAVE (Book #5)
CAUSE TO DREAD (Book #6)

KERI LOCKE MYSTERY SERIES
A TRACE OF DEATH (Book #1)
A TRACE OF MUDER (Book #2)
A TRACE OF VICE (Book #3)
A TRACE OF CRIME (Book #4)
A TRACE OF HOPE (Book #5)

Made in the USA
Monee, IL
06 October 2021